THE TURQUOISE TWINS

Koolidoscope Kids Series ~ Book One

Hiram Taylor & Lorre Brewer

Koolidoscope Content Group ~ New Orleans, La.

Publisher's Cataloging-in-Publication Data

Names: Taylor, Hiram Ed, author. | Brewer, Lorre, 1950- author. Title: The turquoise twins / Hiram Taylor & Lorre Brewer.

Description: Identifiers: Subjects:

New Orleans, LA : Koolidoscope Pictures LLC, [2022] | Series: Koolidoscope kids ; book 1.

ISBN: 978-1-958608-01-2 (paperback) | 978-1-958608-00-5 (ebook) | LCCN: 2022944773

LCSH: Time--Fiction. | Families--Fiction. | Louisiana--Fiction. | Infants--Fiction. | Human skin color--Fiction. | Escapes--Fiction. | Scientists in government--Fiction. | Villains--Fiction. | Mass media--Fiction. | Beauty contestants--Fiction. | Shapeshifting--Fiction.. | LCGFT: Fantasy fiction. | Action and adventure fiction. | Humorous fiction. | BISAC: FICTION / Fantasy / Urban.

Classification: LCC: PS3620.A9445 T87 2022 | DDC: 813.6--dc23

DEDICATION

I want to thank all the people of Louisiana who inspire me with their courage, devotion to life, and great sense of humor even through challenging times. Thanks for the joy, the music, and the rhythm of our language that make us so unique.

-Hiram Taylor-

Contents

Prologue

TIME created Itself, started ticking, and then took a nap.

When TIME awoke, bored, It created a spinning ball of earth to amuse Itself. TIME named him Zordak. Then It took another nap.

TIME dreamed into being the beautiful Vahlmalia, who It created from a breath of air to dance above Zordak. TIME watched their dance until It fell asleep again.

When TIME awoke, Vahlmalia and Zordak were still dancing, and TIME became annoyed and separated her from Zordak, which created friction that caused a fire TIME named Quegor, The Fierce.

TIME swiftly created the swirling diva Aquaria composed of water to calm the flames.

TIME looked at its creations and was pleased but exhausted and thus fell into a deep sleep for an entire week.

The ball kept spinning, the wind kept dancing, the fire kept burning, and the water kept flowing. Balance and harmony in the four Elementals. TIME had just created the heavens and the earth.

Then, TIME created Mankind—and all hell broke loose.

Chapter 1

Arty's Wild Ride

On the day after tomorrow...

Arty Wood, a handsome, rugged young man in his twenties, rode his horse, Mister Jasper, bareback like a free-spirited child on a naughty spree. His long, tousled blond hair blew in the breeze, and his sparkling blue eyes matched the clear skies overhead.

Arty's worn jeans, shrunken from too many washings, were donned with an old shiny belt buckle that his wife's grandpa had handed down. His untucked sleeveless T-shirt matched the brown color of his shiny new cowboy boots, a birthday gift from his famous mom. He looked every inch the movie star cowboy.

Together, the horse and rider galloped over gently rolling hills through a sparsely wooded area in rural Louisiana. Splashing like children, they frolicked in a stream. Then leapt over several fences while still in view of the family farm.

Arty hugged his horse around the neck and spoke to him like a friend. "Okay, Mister Jasper, we'd better head back."

Mister Jasper joyfully disobeyed Arty with a playful toss of his massive head as he swiftly bolted in the opposite direction from home. Arty protested weakly as he had promised his wife, Doreen, he would not venture far from the house because their baby was due at any moment.

As usual, his protests were soon replaced with squeals of delight as Arty and his faithful old friend did what they had done so many times before. The two partners in crime left the present world behind to revisit a magical world of their own. A world that they had created together at a time when Arty was an unbridled towheaded child and Mister Jasper, an unruly colt.

The stallion entered a dark, forbidden sector of the forest where the trees were gigantic. They reached high into the sky like cathedral towers. The bushes were vibrant green and robust. This region felt ancient, almost primeval from a long-lost era. The path was overgrown for a reason. There was an air of magic and wonder, but also something else. Something menacing lurked in the shadows. This space was not to be disturbed by the intrusion of humans.

In olden days, the elders called it the Forbidden Forest. They did not venture where they were not wanted. They told tall tales of fairies, elves, and other creatures, creatures who were sometimes mischievous and those that exuded a sinister aura of mystery.

Sensing something in the bushes ahead that Arty could not see, Mister Jasper halted abruptly. "What's the matter, buddy?" Arty whispered, feeling spooked by the horse's weird behavior.

Mister Jasper's acute instincts sensed that something was amiss. He stood ready to protect his childhood friend from any possible danger that might be lurking in the forest.

Unlike humans, animals trust their intuition. He knew that nefarious creatures existed and hid from view.

Mr. Jasper suspiciously eyed an ancient, gnarled tree surrounded by a cluster of strange greenery that seemed new to him. An incomprehensible being suddenly opened its eyes and stared directly into the eyes of Mister Jasper.

The horse froze, a statue overcome with fear. A chill ran down the horse's spine. He could plainly see what was invisible to Arty.

The massive creature half-monster, half-tree, even a bit human-like in its demeanor was Zordak the elemental who could shape-shift into any earthly form. He was keeping watch on Arty for some unknown reason. Currently he was disguised as a tree. Thick leaves surrounded Zordak's head like a crown. Two limbs grew above his mouth like a heavy mustache. A gaping hole served as a twisted mouth with teeth of twigs opened as if to roar.

Mister Jasper feared that the creature would devour him and Arty alive. How could the stallion know the real reason for Zordak's mysterious appearance? The creature's energy was confusing to the animal but not threatening.

Zordak closed his eyes momentarily to calm the horse and blended right into the tree seeming to disappear. Only to open them quickly as if something had captured his attention. The sudden eye movement caused Mr. Jasper to rear on his hind legs.

Arty could not see the aberration even though he was looking right at him. "Relax old friend there's nothing there" Arty assured the agitated animal lovingly.

The horse was not fooled.

Without warning a huge bolt of silver lightning zigzagged through the mass of trees and struck Zordak. Quegor appeared, the fierce elemental of fire and destruction was Zordak's greatest enemy. Shards of burning wood and flaming leaves flew through the air as the tree exploded into a hundred pieces. Zordak escaped the tree by morphing quickly into a giant stag deer. What had been tree limbs magically turned into giant majestic antlers as the deer deftly vanished into a mist of air provided by Vahlmalia to save Zordak.

The ancient feud between *Time's* elementals had now burst into the world of the human race. They had been hidden for eons from the mind of mankind even though they completely surrounded every man, woman and child all day long. People had taken them for granted as though they did not exist. But they did exist. They had always existed since *Time* made them. The elementals had reached a boiling point, angered by the destruction humans were causing to their world. The Elementals could not agree on a plan, but they were all four determined that in their own way they would make the human race change.

The remains of the tree burst into huge flames as Quegor hissed and sizzled. A smoldering black shadow formed his hideous misshapen humanoid form. He

was composed of shadow, smoke and fire. Quegor
had arrived to thwart the blessed event. An event that
Zordak and Vahlmalia so desperately desired to celebrate
that night. Quegor now turned his wrath towards Arty.

Sensing the evil intentions of the monster, Arty was
jolted into action and jerked on the horse's reins. Mr.
Jasper needed no encouragement, he bolted away in the
opposite direction towards an open field. He was getting
as far away from the tree, the burning man and this
creepy forest as he could gallop.

As they sped away Arty involuntarily shivered. He knew
deep within himself that they had narrowly escaped a
terrible fate. "What was that?" he asked himself out loud
as he tried to shake off the weird encounter.

Mister Jasper jumped over a fallen tree, his hooves
scratched the bark and the horse and rider almost
faltered. Arty came close to falling off, but he held on
tighter now and regained his balance.

But the ferocious Quegor was not finished with them
yet!

Still in the woods, Quegor morphed into black mist and
poured from what was left of the tree. Quegor swirled
into a form that was not human, a walking shadow,
half-man, half-smoking embers.

Quegor took huge steps as he pushed the branches of the scrubs out of his way, they burst into flames. He was leaving a black trail of destruction in his wake. It was no time at all before he stood at the edge of the forest. He came alive with mischievous delight as he pointed his flaming finger at the horse and rider. A shimmering bolt of lightning shot across the field barely missing them.

The horse galloped across the open field at a speed faster than Arty had ever envisioned. His terror evaporated as he focused on the challenge of defeating the lightning. He was sure Mr. Jasper could outrun it. "Go boy! go." It didn't scare Arty, it excited him, it enthralled him. In Arty's reverie, they were suddenly winning a race at the Kentucky Derby. The force of the wind across his face, blew through his hair and forced his eyes to water. It was thrilling. Arty, in his heart, longed for adventure.

Arty's glee suddenly turned to fear as he realized what was happening. He had been hit by lightning before and it was not fun. Quegor's shadow started to grow bigger and higher in a swirl of black and gray fog that suddenly started to fly through the sky towards Arty and his horse.

Quegor laughed and it sounded like booming thunder roaring in Arty's ears. The bolts of lightning zipped from the cloud, flashing across the sky and crashed to the ground in a fury of sizzling silver electricity. The

skillful movements of Mister Jasper managed to evade
the lightning by swirling away from its path, as the horse
jetted across the field like a rocket zooming to Mars.

Another bolt flashed, getting closer, but the horse
dodged it too.

"It's not going to hit us this time," Arty assured his
horse.

Mister Jasper was not listening to Arty. He dodged
relentless bolts of lightning that chased them across the
field. Both rider and horse were sweating from the sheer
exhilaration of the chase and thrill of the moment.

It was just a matter of time before Quegor made a direct
hit.

A mysterious wind picked up around the horse and
rider as Vahlmalia appeared again and morphed into
a gigantic white cloud. She started to fly through the
sky past Quegor towards Arty and his horse protecting
him by blocking the lightning bolts. Her clouds were so
thick they blocked Quegor's vision. He cursed at her
and vaporized himself into a gigantic ball of flames and
disappeared.

The horse and rider were on the final leg of the day's
adventure. Mister Jasper was clearly in charge as he

headed for the finish line. He gave a sly backward glance over his shoulder at Arty as he prepared to cap off the day with a grand finale. Arty braced himself, knowing anything could happen.

Arty, seeing Grandpa's tall, slim figure bent over working on his tractor, attempted to rein in his horse to circumvent any potential mishap. He knew Grandpa had lost his hearing when he was a fighter pilot in the war.

"Whoa boy, take it eeeeeeeeeeee zeeee Whoaaaaah."

The horse picked up the pace even more as he made a bee-line towards the barn and farmhouse where he could see Grandpa working on his tractor in the distance.

Unaware of what was barreling toward him, Grandpa expertly fixed his old 1960's model tractor with a wrench and the determination of a family doctor operating on a good friend. Grandpa knew what he was doing from his years of working as a mechanic on jeeps and airplanes in the military.

Grandpa's dog and constant companion Ol' Blue yawned lazily as he lay sprawled on top of Grandpa's tools. Grandpa lifted up Blue's backside to retrieve a different wrench. Ol' Blue protested weakly and gave a half-hearted howl and set his paw on the correct wrench

with a smug self-satisfied grunt. Grandpa shook his head
and replied with a half-signed, half-dismissive gesture.
The Blue Tick Coonhound snorted. Blue knew he was
the master of this farm where he had been born.

Ol' Blue sniffed the air and suddenly bounded off the
tool table with a wild wail. The sudden change of
weather and the vibration of the approaching horse and
rider had set off Blue's protective antenna.

In the pasture behind the barn a herd of red cows were
grazing in the field when Mister Jasper leapt over the
barbed wire fence. They stopped eating and watched
as the horse and Arty swept past them, then calmly,
unfazed, went back to eating.

Grandpa looked up just in time to see the pair racing
towards him. He wiped his oily hands on his overalls.
His weathered face that had been crinkled up in
concentration as he worked immediately broke into a
semi-toothless grin. A chuckle escaped his lips. The years
dropped away revealing the mischievous imp he had
been since birth. He smiled as his twinkling green eyes
danced.

Grandpa's attention was drawn away by the black cloud
above in the sky. The sudden bolts of lightning seemed
to be targeting the horse and rider as they sped past him.

Arty and Mister Jasper passed Grandpa as the horse raced full speed towards the door of the barn. The dark cloud magically evaporated into mist and disappeared.

When Mister Jasper reached the barn door, the horse reared and stopped short, causing Arty to fly off into a pile of hay.

Arty saw something moving in the hay in front of the horse. He crawled over on his hands and knees as both of them stared down at a mama cat, Miss Tootsie, and her newborn kittens.

Arty's face filled with compassion as he stared at the pile of little yellow meowing babies, their eyes still not open. Miss Tootsie licked them lovingly, one by one.

"Aw, look, Mister Jasper, Miss Tootsie had her babies. Aren't they cute?"

Mister Jasper whinnied in reply. His hide was wet with sweat from their wild gallop across the field. Arty patted his horse lovingly, then looked at his wet hand. "We're both soaked, aren't we?" Arty laughed and wiped his hands on his jeans. "That was one wild ride. Thanks for stopping, or we'd have run right over the kittens. I think we should move them out of the door, don't you?"

The horse shook his head yes. But, when Arty tried to help the cat, she hissed.

"Miss Tootsie, we need to move you out of the door a bit." He tried, but the cat was not moving. She hissed at him again, holding her ground. He reacted and pulled away.

"Well, okay, I guess you're staying where you are, aren't ya?" He said to the cat, then talked to the horse as he stood. "No use arguing with a new mama."

The horse nodded in agreement again. There was something almost childlike in the way Arty talked to his animals. They were his friends, and he loved them.

"Let me get some lights on in here, so nobody else stumbles on top of your babies."

Arty went to the light switch. Sparks of electricity flew from his fingers as the lightbulbs in the barn flashed on and off.

The cat looked worried. The horse looked worried.

"Don't worry. I got this," he assured them.

They did not believe him, and both prepared for the worst.

When Arty touched the light switch, all the light bulbs exploded and set the hay on fire.

Arty ran and grabbed a fire extinguisher. He hosed everything around him, spraying white stuff all over the place, including the cats and horse.

Immediately, Miss Tootsie grabbed one of her kittens by the nape of their neck and, one by one, moved them all to a safer place away from the white foam. The horse shook himself vigorously, trying to get rid of the goop covering him. They weren't happy, but the fire was out.

Suddenly there was a loud scream from the farmhouse.

Chapter 2

The Miracle

The scream came from Doreen, Arty's very pregnant wife. She burst through the back door with a bang and rushed out from the kitchen onto the small wooden back porch. She was huffing and puffing, taking deep, long breaths.

In between breaths, she leaned against the porch post and struggled to jam her feet into her army boots. She was charmingly disheveled, wearing a short cotton dress covered by a green combat jacket. Her dark hair tumbled around her face in cascading ringlets. Doreen was as beautiful as a beauty queen and as full of energy as a stick of exploding dynamite.

"Arty!" She screamed loudly. She stopped, grabbed her protruding stomach, and yelled again. "Arty!"

Arty rushed out of the barn, concerned. He was still covered in white stuff like a snowman. "Doreen, honey, you alright?" He started wiping himself clean with a horse blanket.

She calmed down and quickly answered him. "Arty, sugar, this baby has decided. Now is the time. Do ya hear me? Now is the time."

Arty did not seem to understand her, he was still more excited about the birth of the kittens. "Miss Tootsie had her kittens right there in the hay."

Doreen shook her head in dismay and started down the rickety old wooden steps holding onto the wooden rail as carefully as she could manage. She was used to jumping over land mines instead of waddling down the stairs like a duck and headed over to the pickup truck.

She was so uncomfortable at this point in the pregnancy. She couldn't sleep because of her distorted body shape. She could barely get up and down from a stupid chair—she was so over this.

"I'm going to have our baby right here in the dirt if you don't get over here and help me." She threatened sarcastically.

"Just a minute." He replied.

"I don't think we got a minute."

Arty now realized she meant it and saw how she was struggling. He rushed over to help her. When he touched her, it shocked her. She recoiled in pain.

"Ouch! You're all electrified again. Stay away from me, you Zapper."

Arty was horrified that he had zapped her. He quickly put his hands behind his back and tried desperately to explain.

"Static electricity, that's all. I can't help it."

Doreen gave him a knowing look. "Did you get hit by lightning again?"

"No, it missed us. Mister Jasper outran it."

The horse whinnied and shook his head.

"Thank the lord for that horse." She threw Mister Jasper a kiss, then struggled so hard that Arty tried to help her again. She jumped and pushed his hand away.

"Don't touch me—stay away."

He did. But getting into the battered old truck was quite an ordeal for her. Arty kept his distance but felt upset that he couldn't help her.

Suddenly out of nowhere, a flash of lightning zigzagged across the yard, narrowly missing Arty as he jumped in horror. Quegor was at it again with the lightning. It started pouring rain. This time, Aquaria was helping by becoming a storm. Arty ran to the barn, led the horse inside, and closed the door.

Doreen looked at him exasperated, "what are you doing now?"

"I don't want the kittens to get wet."

"Are you kidding me?"

Grandpa ran towards the house and started up the stairs to get out of the rain. He saw Doreen struggling to get into the front seat of the truck. He came over to her and signed, "Can I help?"

She emphatically signed back to him, "The baby is coming." He nodded and understood, then smiled and calmly helped steady her.

"Oh, Grandpa, I forgot my lucky necklace. You know the one Mama made me with the man and the woman on it. It's on the sink in the bathroom. Tell Mama to bring it to the hospital." She signed hurriedly to Grandpa. No need, he had read her lips.

She waved bye-bye to Grandpa, who ran out of the rain and into the house, forgetting to close Doreen's truck door. She reached over and tried to close it, but it was impossible. She called her husband. "Arty, will you come close my door? Grandpa forgot." Arty raced around to shut it. Doreen looked at him and laid down the law. "We just got to get us a car, sugar. No child of mine is going to be riding in the back of this piece of junk like some gun-totin' hick." He nodded in agreement.

Doreen screamed again in pain and grabbed her belly while she kept taking deep breaths. Arty, standing in the rain like a timid puppy, desperately wanted to help but didn't know how.

"Can't I do something?" He asked.

"Drive!"

"Oh, yeah."

He ran around and jumped into the truck behind the steering wheel. Doreen looked down at his muddy shoes.

"Well, ain't we gonna look like hillbilly farmers with you bringing half the field in that clean hospital on those muddy shoes?"

Arty tried to start the motor, but sparks flew out of his hand when he turned the key. Doreen sighed and shook her head. "Must I do everything? Next time you're having the baby, I'll drive."

Arty jumped out of the truck and started around to the passenger side as Doreen struggled to squeeze under the steering wheel with the baby bump.

She talked to the baby, "Come on, sugar dumpling, tight fit, but daddy zapped the truck, and mama has got to drive."

Arty was about halfway around the truck when a lightning bolt hit him. He sizzled. He thought he heard a strange masculine laugh. His body shook uncontrollably as he stumbled and twisted his way to the door of the truck, opened it, and slowly got in.

She looked at him, amazed that this had happened again. "How many times now does that make?"

He staggered and shook his way into the seat. His voice quivered and stuttered as he tried to answer. "Eighteen." he finally managed to say.

She smiled and felt such deep love for him. She wanted to comfort him in his misery, but she was afraid to touch him yet.

"You're just electrifyin', sweetheart." She slowly took his hand and put it on her belly. Arty reacted but didn't pull away.

"I don't want to shock the baby."

"It's okay. Baby likes it. Sometimes Mama does too." She assured him. She hit the gas pedal, and the truck flew down the driveway and out onto the road.

"Doreen, you're gonna be the world's greatest mama."

The pickup truck continued down the rural Louisiana road in what looked like the middle of nowhere, endless sugarcane fields on one side and cow pastures on the other. They passed a big weather-beaten sign that read in large colorful letters Welcome to Rainbow City, but no city was in sight, just more fields. This was backwoods farm country.

Inside the cab of the truck, Arty still held his hand on Doreen's stomach, comforting the baby as she drove.

The rain was heavier, and she could barely see through the window as the squeaky wipers struggled to keep a spot clean. Then she suddenly saw something move, as a cow headed across the road in front of the truck.

Arty yelled, "Watch out for that cow"

"What cow?" she yelled back at him.

Arty grabbed the wheel to keep the truck from hitting the animal.

"That cow."

The truck slid off the road and into a muddy ditch. The cow stopped, stood in the middle of the road in the headlights, and looked at them as if to say, "What the—?"

"Now ya done it," Doreen told Arty.

She tried to drive back onto the road, but the tires spun and sank deeper into the mud. "We're stuck," she groaned.

Arty got out of the truck to assess the situation. The tires were buried deep into the soggy dirt. The cow came over and looked too.

"Would it help if I push?" Arty asked Doreen. The cow shook her head yes.

Doreen rolled down the window and shouted at him from inside. "Do something!"

Arty went behind the truck and got ready to push. "Let her rip," he shouted to Doreen.

Doreen gunned the motor. The tires spewed mud all over Arty. The truck only went deeper.

Doreen crawled out of the truck and came around to view the situation. She was hopping mad. She doubled over in agony. By now, the labor pains were coming every two minutes.

The cow looked over the situation, too, then mooed loudly.

"Oh, shut up. You were almost roadkill." Doreen snapped. The cow immediately gave her a look. Arty apologized to the cow.

"She didn't mean that. She's in labor, having a baby." Then he whispered to the cow. "She's hormonal."

Doreen growled "I—am—not—hormonal!"

Arty looked at the cow and whispered, "She's hormonal." The cow responded with a knowing moo as she started walking down the road. "She says to follow her. There's a barn nearby."

Arty pulled Doreen, and they followed the cow. Doreen was getting even more hysterical. "I don't need a barn; I need a hospital."

Arty tried to comfort her. "Let's get inside where it's dry, and I'll call the hospital."

"I was dry in the truck," she insisted.

They followed the cow into the barn, where there were many other cows. Some were feeding at the troughs, and others were chewing hay from several bales stacked around.

Arty greeted them. "Hello, everyone." A couple of cows mooed in response. But most of the herd could care less.

Doreen leaned into Arty's ear and asked him in a whisper. "What did they say? Are we welcome?"

"Yes. We are." He assured her.

She was relieved and finally relaxed a bit. He led her to a bale of hay and helped her as she struggled to an uncomfortable sitting position.

He got out his cell phone and tried to call the hospital. "No bars." He explained, "I'll try outside."

Doreen was still struggling to balance herself on the bale of hay that the cow was slowly eating. Finally, she turned to it and asked, "Do you mind eating a different bale?"

The cow took one last bite, chewing on the string holding the bale together. Then, she jerked it gently, so the bale opened, and Doreen was able to lay back more comfortably. Doreen was surprised.

"Whoa! Thank you, that's much better." Very pleased and satisfied with herself, the cow mooed again and walked away to graze with the other cows.

Arty exited the barn doors back outside into the rain. He shivered as he made his call. "Can you hear me now?"

Unseen by Arty, a very bright blue star twinkled above the barn in the night sky. Suddenly, it seemed to be getting closer and closer and brighter and brighter as it moved toward him. It was Vahlmalia watching over them.

Arty did not notice it at all. He was too busy explaining his situation to the emergency operator at the hospital.

"She is in labor. We're not far, about two miles down from the Fatboy Donut factory on Old Bayou Road. We're in a cow barn right across from the Welcome to Rainbow City sign. Please hurry."

Doreen shrieked. "These babies are ready to pop out now!"

Arty rushed inside to her.

"The ambulance is on the way," Arty explained as he ran over to Doreen.

"So are the babies. You are going to have to deliver them."

"Me? I don't know nothin' 'bout birthin' babies."

"Get down there and pretend it's a football and catch it."

"Catch the football. I can do that." Arty agreed.

He got into position, down between her legs, ready to catch the football.

"It's coming!" screamed Doreen

"I see the baby," Arty assured her. His eyes filled with excitement and delight.

The parents were unaware of what was happening around them as the barn filled with a luminous energy. Vahlmalia's bright, shimmering blue light had magically descended through the roof and surrounded them. It emitted a glow that was the transparent image of the beautiful blue elemental Vahlmalia. Her dress was made of a flowing mass of twinkling stars. Her glimmering body created a heavenly canopy protecting this enchanted birth from all that might harm from above.

Below her, several twigs of green vines started to spontaneously sprout out of the ground, followed by a bushy mass of tree leaves that were like hair as the hands and then the head and face of Zordak emerged. His green tree-like leafy figure spread the entire length of the floor protecting the birth from all that would harm from below.

Zordak stretched his arms above his head as branches and twigs grew from his arms and feet that reached for the sky.

Simultaneously at each end of the canopy of light, Vahlmalia reached down from above to meet Zordak's branches that were reaching to the heavens. Zordak supporting from below and Vahlmalia protecting from above.

When the green branches met the blue stars, they tenderly came together in an embrace, swaying, then rotating gently, then twirling exuberantly. The green man and the beautiful blue vision joyfully danced together, creating a whirling vortex mixing blue and green that blended into a stunning turquoise light that flooded Arty and Doreen in a magical glow. Soon it filled the entire barn.

Arty called out in the excitement of the moment. "I got it! So now, what do I do?"

"Catch the other one!" Doreen wailed.

Arty exhaled, "I got it."

In the distance, an ambulance flew down the road with its flashing light. It turned into the field and headed for the barn.

The flashing red light and the bright headlights of the ambulance shined into the barn.

Vahlmalia's light rescinded back into space as it shone down on the barn from above. Zordak's body of leaves and twigs faded back into the ground.

Two medics in light green shirts and dark green pants jumped out of the ambulance and headed into the barn with their flashlights. They found Arty passed out on the ground. Then, they heard a giggling sound and flashed their lights on Doreen. She was sitting in the pile of hay holding two giggling, happy, turquoise babies.

TIME was puzzled and decided to sleep on it.

Chapter 3

Monsters Within

The picturesque Alpine scenery in the beautiful Smoky Mountains of Tennessee was marred by the sight of a massive, creepy black hole drilled into the side of the mountain. Enormous concrete boulders lined the entrance. Heavy barbed wire fencing ran along the two-lane blacktop road leading into the hole. A red sports car drove up the mountain road and disappeared into the giant black cave.

Inside, it pulled into the main section of a secret military base hidden inside the mountain. The compound was solid gray concrete, sterile and lifeless, except for one man.

A young soldier named Private Harper was standing at attention, waiting for the car's arrival. The car screeched to a halt. Doctor Victor Wood, a devil in an expensive suit, slithered out like a coiled poisonous snake.

Victor had an amazing resemblance to Arty. They were identical twins; except they were complete opposites. Victor was suave, smooth, sure of himself, ruthless, and cruel.

Young Harper saluted and groveled to his superior. Victor got out of his car and saluted back.

"At ease Harper." He threw the car keys at Harper, who caught them with ease. Victor barked out orders to him. "Proceed with Operation Lockdown."

Harper saluted. "Yes, sir."

He got in Victor's car, drove it across the concrete pavement only a few feet away, and parked it.

A heavily tattooed, gum-chewing, pink-haired woman in a nurse's uniform, Nurse Winebombs, rushed up to Victor as if the world had come to an end. She had been through the wringer of life a few times and lost some of her marbles.

She saluted. "Doctor Wood, sir," Winebombs asked for permission to speak.

Victor saluted back but with an attitude. "At ease, Winebombs. What is it?"

"Sir, Operation Baby Drop Gumbo has blown sky high down in Louisiana, Sir. All signals off the chart. The motherlode has dropped the payload."

"Speak English Winebombs."

"She had twins, and they are—turquoise."

Victor smiled. He was very pleased. "How marvelous. If music be the food of love, play on."

He waited for her to answer. She thought for a moment, then made a guess. It was a game they played. One she obviously hated.

"The Beatles, sir?" She asked timidly, afraid, expecting to be yelled at.

Victor rolled his eyes in disgust, "Shakespeare, *Twelfth Night,* opening line—you imbecile!"

Winebombs winced in pain, almost as if he had beaten her with a stick. "Sorry, sir."

He was very stern, very stern indeed in his reply. "Haven't you been listening to those paraliminal mind-expanding programs I prescribed to broaden your feeble mind?"

She stuttered and stammered excuses. "Well, with Operation Baby Drop Gumbo and all the plans, the plane, setting up the—"

He cut her off. "—No more excuses, Winebombs. You must expand your mind if you want to play games with a genius like me. Otherwise, I will have to find a new assistant."

"Yes, sir, no sir, I won't, sir. I mean, I will. Whatever you say, Sir." she managed to fumble through with no grace.

Two orderlies, an obese slob, nicknamed Fat Sam, and a dimwit beanpole named Trumbo, pulled a struggling blond towards Victor and Winebombs. She was Miss Dana LaFoosie, dressed in a fabulous designer ball gown and expensive jewels. She was obviously once a somebody that nobody cared about nowadays but Victor.

When Victor saw her, he turned on all his charm and weaseled his way over to her.

"Oh, darling, Dana LaFoosie, you look divine. I got us tickets to the opera tonight. *Madam Butterfly.* I know it's a bore, but the President insists we be there..."

Winebombs panicked and cut him off "—But Operation Baby Drop Gumbo, sir."

Victor was beside himself with anger at being interrupted. He turned on Winebombs with a scowl on his face, and his fingers curled like a tiger ready to scratch her throat out.

"How dare you speak while I am speaking to this famous former game show hostess whom I have adored since I was a child. Insubordination will not be tolerated."

Winebombs would not be stopped. "But she's had the babies, sir, twins. We must go now."

Victor paid no attention to Winebombs. He walked away from her, calmed himself, and returned to the men holding Dana. He continued speaking. "My dear Miss LaFoosie, please forgive the rude interruption; there will be a marvelous dinner afterward and..." before he could say more, Dana vomited on him, a purple puke. He recoiled in disgust from the foul smell and quickly took off his jacket and handed it to Winebombs.

"What's wrong with her?" He asked Trumbo.

"She tried eating raw eggplants again," Trumbo answered.

Victor exploded, "Again? I detest such cheap sentiment. I thought she was cured once and for always of desiring purple food."

Dana started foaming at the mouth, bright purple foam; it dropped down on Fat Sam.

"She's drooling purple stuff on me, uh, sir. Is it contagious?" Fat Sam cried out like a baby.

Victor rolled his eyes, "Oh, alright. Hook her up to Ol' Lightning and give her another treatment."

"Wez gonna juice her in dat machine?" Fat Sam stuttered in horror.

"You heard me snap to it. Don't stand there like numbskulls!"

The men dragged Dana through electric double doors into the main building of Doctor Wood's Experimental Laboratory. Victor started to follow them, but Winebombs grabbed him and desperately tried to steer him in the opposite direction.

"The plane is ready and waiting. It is now or never for Operation Baby Drop Gumbo, sir." She pleaded.

Victor tried calming himself by taking deep breaths as he led her towards the door. "Breathe, Winebombs. Everything is perfect in this best of all possible worlds."

She stopped dead in her tracks. She was stuck. Oh, she hated this game. She guessed again, "*The Secret? The Law of Attraction,* Sir*?*"

He exploded. "Voltaire!"

Winebombs winced and wrinkled her face in despair. She never got any of the answers right. It drove her insane. She hated listening to those boring tapes as they put her to sleep. But she tried so hard to please her master. She really wanted to please him.

He rushed into the building without her. She reluctantly followed him, knowing that when Operation Baby Drop Gumbo blew up in their face, Victor would blame her, and it was not her fault. Still, it was her who would be punished.

The interior hallway to Victor's lab was more like a maze in a carnival ride nightmare than a military hospital. Screams echoed from a series of rooms down a long hallway that looked very much like a weirdly designed mental ward of a low-budget horror movie.

Victor looked into several large glass windows with extreme curiosity as he passed but then proceeded down the hallway without venturing inside. He followed the men ahead. They struggled with Dana. Suddenly, Victor stopped before one of the rooms and peered inside.

A deranged male patient sat strapped into a heavy chair bolted to the floor. There were many wires hooked to his head that were attached to several machines with beeping sounds and red, yellow, and blue flashing lights. The patient seemed to be in a high state of extreme fear. He was shaking with it, sweat pouring over his tightly bound mouth, which blocked the sound of his obvious screaming. The blood vessels on his face were popping out across his forehead and looked like any minute they would explode.

Victor opened the door and asked, "Everything okay in here, Doctor Bobo?"

An elderly, overweight man in a white lab coat stood at a coffee station. He observed the experiment while drinking coffee in a paper cup.

"Yes, I am curing this poor man, one Private Leroy
Purvis, of his fear brought on from watching those alien
movies." Doctor Bobo explained, "By making him relive
the moment at the root of his fear, the opening of the
pods." He pointed to the scene in front of him, where
the patient sat watching several strange pods oozing
slimy stuff slowly as they opened.

It was clear the man in the chair was desperately pleading
with Victor to save him. Victor paid him no mind.
Victor seemed impressed as he closed the door. "Very
good, Doctor Bobo; keep up the good work."

Suddenly, a spurt of the gooey stuff flew across the
room and attached itself to the patient's face. Leroy went
berserk as the chair banged on the floor. The beeping
became extremely rapid as the lights began flashing faster
and faster. Doctor Bobo looked bored as he sipped his
coffee and glanced at his watch.

Victor and Winebombs moved further down the hall.
Fat Sam and Trumbo had taken Dana into the last room
at the end of the hallway.

Suddenly, a door opened, and a wild wolf in a sequin
gown ran out, growling and clawing gashes into the tile
floor as it struggled to escape. A nurse was chasing it with
an unusual hypodermic needle. She quickly injected a
glowing substance into the animal that howled a loud
painful cry. Then, before their eyes, the beast changed
back to beauty. The long fangs, brightly polished pink,

turned into feminine fingernails that still clawed on the tile floor as the nurse dragged a beautiful brunette woman back into the room and closed the door.

Victor turned to Winebombs and asked, "A new patient?"

"A former Miss America, Bitzy Bloom, with rage issues."

"I wonder what her talent was?"

Winebombs looked at her chart. "Dramatic monologue, Lady Macbeth."

Victor smiled. "The *out damn spot scene*, I suppose." he chuckled, "Interesting choice for a werewolf."

They arrived at their final destination, Victor's main lab. Usually, it was just called *Victor's Playroom* by the staff. It was filled with lots of weird futuristic space-age torture devices, a real Doctor Frankenstein house of horrors. The main attraction was in a caged area, where a monstrous, incredible machine was spinning sparks of various colors of lightning bolts into the air. It buzzed and hissed in a large crystal globe.

Victor thought it was very impressive. To the feeble-minded like Fat Sam and Trumbo, it was scary. Doctor Bobo thought it was *camp*. He giggled about it behind Victor's back. Winebombs knew Victor was proud of his creation, and so was she.

"Put Miss LaFoosie in the machine. Strap her in tight, boys." Victor demanded in a Vincent Price sort of way. Victor loved old horror movies, and the United States government was paying him big money to live one in real life.

The men dragged Dana into the metal cage surrounding the astronomic machine. Victor was enjoying himself as he loved to play torture master with his patients. The more gruesome and scarier it was, the better it worked on their twisted minds.

Fat Sam seemed very nervous. It was his first day on the job, and he was trying to make a good impression, but this seemed a little more than he had signed up for. "In dere?" He asked, pointing at the machine. "What's dis thang do?"

"It rearranges the molecular structure of the brain," Trumbo answered very matter-of-factly.

Fat Sam was terrified. "Dis twern't in no job 'scription," he mumbled.

"You wanna get paid?" Trumbo asked.

Fat Sam could not argue with that. They strapped Dana into the machine. Trumbo quickly pushed Fat Sam out of the way, ran past him, and locked the gate to the cage, leaving Fat Sam inside. His face filled with fear. Fat Sam banged on the bars of the cage, desperately begging for them to show him mercy.

"Wet me out!" he screamed, terrified. They were all laughing by this time, enjoying his fear.

Down the hall in Doctor Bobo's room, Leroy continued struggling with the thing on his face. Doctor Bobo busied himself looking through a small refrigerator. Finally, he spotted what he was looking for and took a box of jelly donuts out of the fridge. He opened the box and squeezed several to see what flavor hid inside. He put the chocolate, the raspberry, and the cherry ones all aside until he found the right one—lemon.

His eyes glowed with excitement. He paid no attention to Leroy behind him who was going completely insane over the alien thing plastered on his face.

Doctor Bobo picked up the jelly donut like it was a prize and bit into it with delight and satisfaction. Yellow goo dripped from his lips as he licked it with his tongue. He gobbled the entire donut down quickly. Burped. And waited.

At his mouth, the yellow goo started to flow out of him. It poured out of each ear. It covered his face. It ran down his leg until his entire body was a humongous glob of lemon jelly.

The Glob started creeping across the floor. The sweet, tangy chemical smell of artificial lemon flavoring filled the air.

Leroy, still in the chair, sensed something. His eyes looked in Doctor Bobo's direction and caught sight of the enormous glob of yellow goo inching towards him. He went even more berserk as he saw The Glob coming at him. His eyes widened in even more terror, so wide they appeared ready to pop out of their sockets. The Glob wobbled right past him. It plopped against the glass window, then slowly rolled down and oozed under the lab door and out into the hallway. Leroy passed out cold.

Meanwhile, in Victor's lab, Fat Sam was still banging furiously on the cage bars and praying to heaven. He knew he would soon be dead; he just knew it. Trumbo, Winebombs, and Victor were still laughing and enjoying the poor man's prayers. Victor pushed a red button and the glass dome opened slowly. Fat Sam stopped praying and turned his face in horror at the sight. The lightning was flashing bolts of electricity into Dana's body. She struggled and twisted and screamed.

Victor stood calmly, almost bored by the procedure, with a stopwatch in his hand. "Oh, such a fuss," he uttered.

In the cage, Dana began to turn into a purple mega-monster. She was getting bigger and bigger until she broke loose from her chain bindings. Giant wings burst from her back. Her face stretched and elongated like a dragon.

Fat Sam stood frozen in fear as she approached him. "She's a purple people eater!" He screamed, pleading again for mercy.

"Don't worry; she won't hurt you. She only eats purple people." Victor declared as he started to laugh again and thought to himself, this was a better show than any old opera.

Dana's bright pink, extremely long tongue crept slowly through the air until it reached Fat Sam's cheek. She innocently licked Fat Sam's face like a puppy. Her gigantic wings wrapped around him as she gave him a sweet loving hug. He screamed anyway.

Victor turned to Trumbo. "Juice her another ten thousand volts every hour on the hour until she stabilizes back to her normal self."

"Yes, sir," Trumbo snapped to attention.

Winebombs marched over to Victor and plopped a computer in front of him. The show was over, and this time she meant business.

"Stats off the chart already, Sir. We should have infiltrated Rainbow City by now and set up shop. We may be forced to liquidate innocent bystanders to capture those turquoise twins and bring them back here for testing and observation."

Victor snapped his stopwatch and put it in his pocket. "Relax, Winebombs. She has a playmate now and will be back to her old self in no time. Now, we can go."

They turned towards the door and saw yellow goo oozing under the door behind them. It grew larger and larger until it became The Glob again.

"Oh, how charming, a goodbye, friendly sendoff visit from The Glob," Victor snickered with a grin on his face.

Winebombs saw it and was not pleased. As it inched towards her, she grabbed a fire extinguisher and sprayed it. "Doctor Bobo, this is no time for such nonsense. We're already late."

The goo transformed back into Doctor Bobo. He stood there as his usual self. "I was just having a little fun. Everyone's getting so stuffy around here."

Victor again spoke to Trumbo. "Make sure there are no more lemon jelly donuts anywhere on this base."

"Oh, that's not nice." Doctor Bobo whined.

"Come, Winebombs, to the plane. The rest of you are on high alert in case we need you." Victor declared as he exited with Winebombs.

Doctor Bobo continued to whine to himself. "And he used to be such a charming fellow."

Chapter 4

Crawfish Queen

The ambulance pulled up to a small rural hospital emergency room. Built in the bustling economy of the 1960's it had become a bit rundown in the fifty years of service to this shrinking town in central Louisiana. The flower beds were more weeds than flowers. The concrete ramps were filled with wide cracks. The automatic doors weren't automatic anymore and often needed a good hard shove to force them open. Still, this town was lucky to have a hospital. So many towns' hospitals had closed down due to budget cuts.

Sally Ann Dingledorper, a child beauty queen wore her tiara in an over teased beehive hairdo. Her face covered in garish adult makeup made her look forty. She was probably eight or nine years old. Sally Ann stomped her feet as her tap shoes made a loud clunking sound on the tile floor. "I'll have you know I am the Little Miss Crawfish Queen of Louisiana, and I'm having a traumatic episode, and I need my medication—*now.*"

She struck a dramatic pose and waited for a response from a young woman receptionist who was madly texting on her phone. Sally Ann dropped her pose. "Are you listening to me? I'll call my daddy"

The receptionist could care less, she had these type people in here before, and she just continued texting. "You'll have to wait your turn like everyone else," she murmured in a monotone voice.

"Queens don't wait turns." Sally Ann reached into a baby doll carriage with two well-worn dolls and retrieved her inhaler. Then took two blasts of the medicinal mist into her lungs. "You'll regret this." She threatened the receptionist with a newly found sharp, evil voice. She took one of the dolls, removed a hairpin from her beehive, and pushed it into the doll's head. The receptionist jumped and grabbed her head in pain, unaware of where the pain came from. Sally Ann cackled as she laid the doll down into the carriage and pulled out a small purse and opened it. She dug around inside until she pulled out a tube of red lipstick and a compact. She touched up her makeup and admired herself in the round mirror.

Nurse Feelgoode, a jolly, middle-aged lady, came rushing up to the receptionist behind the counter and whispered. "She's the little girl who fed the poor Parker boy rat poison. I'd be careful if I was you. It's a miracle he didn't die. No telling what she may do to you if you make her angry."

Sally Ann heard her and gave them both the evil eye. "I did my time."

"They just let her out of the mental institution," whispered Nurse Feelgoode, "I'd get her those pills if I was you."

Sally Ann marched over to the main doors just as they crashed open without warning. She jumped back. "This place is a deathtrap!" She screamed, "Someone oughta bulldoze it down."

The medics rolled Doreen, still holding the babies, into the room; Arty followed behind.

Sally Ann saw the babies before anyone else in the room. She announced to the world in a booming voice, "Those babies are blue!"

A nurse holding a clipboard with admittance papers walked over. At first, she paid no attention to the babies, then, when she saw their color, she screamed, dropped her clipboard, and ran out.

The medics rolled Doreen through different doors into the main hospital.

Arty did not get through the doors quick enough and was stuck in the waiting room. "But I'm with them. I'm the father," he insisted, pounding on the doors. He turned and looked at the people in the room who were staring at him. He had forgotten how dirty he was from the mud of the road which covered half his face. Large clumps of hay were hanging from his filthy long hair. His jeans and boots were covered in mud. No one quite knew what to make of him.

Sally Ann, furious that no one was paying attention to her, demanded the spotlight back. "I said those babies are blue—blue as Tupperware bowls—they must be aliens." Sally Ann declared.

Everyone in the room screamed at once. "Aliens!"

Sally Ann quickly reached into her doll carriage again, pulled out a cell phone, and dialed. "Get me the newsroom quick. Aliens have invaded the hospital here in Rainbow City," she blurted into the phone, as she flipped her hair and struck another dramatic pose. She performed as much for the audience in the room as for the person answering the phone at the local radio station. "This is Sally Ann Dingledorper, and I'm at the hospital where two blue aliens were just brought into the emergency room."

Arty could not stand it anymore. He headed out towards the parking lot. Outside, Arty saw Doreen's mother and Grandpa headed toward him. He wished the earth would open below him and he could escape into a hole because he was so dirty.

Doreen's mother, Thelma Lou, saw him and ran over. "There's Arty." She pointed and signed for Grandpa, who now saw Arty too.

Thelma Lou looked and acted like a perky poodle. She was nervous, fidgety, and constantly barking orders to Arty in a high-pitched voice as she signed for Grandpa at the same time. Her dark brown hair matched the color of her eyes. It was a tightly curled haircut popular with middle-aged ladies in the South. But Arty remembered it being more popular in Hollywood on poodles.

"Oh, my word Arty, I was so worried. We passed your old truck in the ditch on the road, and I thought to myself, oh my word, Arty had a wreck." Finally pausing long enough to catch her breath, she asked. "Is Doreen okay?"

"She's fine. I called an ambulance."

"Thank god." She was relieved until she suddenly saw how dirty Arty was. "Oh, Arty, you look like you rolled around in a mud puddle. What happened?"

"You don't wanna know." He answered.

"Is Doreen still in labor?"

"Oh, no. The babies are here."

Thelma Lou was shocked. "Babies? Did you say, babies?"

"Yes. twins."

She quickly signed for Grandpa. He got very excited. "We've got to see them." They rushed past him into the main hospital. "Be sure to wash up, don't track all that mud into this clean hospital." She instructed Arty back over her shoulder.

"Yes, ma'am," Arty sighed.

Thelma Lou and Grandpa went inside.

Arty turned and saw a red sports car pull into the parking lot. He trembled like a child caught with his hand in the cookie jar. The car's brakes squealed as it slammed to a quick stop. The door opened, and a voluptuous blond woman, Bambi Wood, swept out of the car flamboyantly.

"Oh my gosh, Mama." Arty groaned out loud to himself, looking down at his dirty clothes.

As she got closer, Bambi appeared in all her glory to be the fabulous movie star that she always was on screen. Her face was flawless, her hair perfect, and her manner grand. She looked much too young to be a grandmother. She rushed up to him to hug him, then pulled back in shock.

"Arty, darling, you look like a pig farmer. Don't kiss me. This dress is Chanel."

Arty kept his distance but could really have used a hug. Instead, he walked over to a water hose in a flower bed and hosed himself clean. Bambi was horrified. She watched him from a distance.

Arty shivered from the cold water as it rushed over him.

"This is not the life I raised you for. Why couldn't you be more like your brother? He's a world-famous doctor of something or other, and you are—"

Arty finished her sentence, "—a pig farmer, we don't have any pigs. We have cows, cats, chickens, a rooster, a dog Ol' Blue and Mister Jasper."

"I know, darling, but he's rich and successful."

"Like you." He added as he finished up his washing by wringing out his hair.

"Well, no one is as rich and successful as me, darling, and so you are *not* a farmer; you are an agriculture specialist. At least that's what I tell the press in New York and L.A. when I'm on the red carpet. They always ask about you because you were so cute in your little tuxedo when you escorted me to the Oscars. Look at you now? Thank God there's no press around. When is this baby due?"

"The babies have arrived." He announced proudly.

She was shocked. "Babies? Not twins, I hope. Twins run in our family like arthritis."

"Not only are they twins, Mama. They are a weird color. They're strange."

She looked at him confused and worried. "What do you mean, strange?"

"You'll see," he said as he tried to escort her inside, leaving a flow of dirty water on the pavement behind him.

"Stay away," she insisted as she hurried ahead of him.

At the same time, Thelma Lou and Grandpa entered Doreen's hospital room with big smiles on their faces that instantly dropped when they saw Doreen in bed holding the babies. Doreen was overjoyed to see her family.

"Mama, Grandpa," she exclaimed. "Look at my beautiful babies."

For once in her life, Thelma Lou was speechless, her mouth moved, but no words came out. Thelma Lou dropped the beloved necklace depicting the blue woman and the green man that Doreen had asked Grandpa to bring her.

Grandpa picked up the necklace and signed something to Doreen as he handed it to her. "Oh, my necklace" She put it around her neck. "Yes, Grandpa. They're turquoise twins. We haven't named them yet, but I want to call my little girl Willow because I think she is graceful like a tree. If it were a boy, Arty wanted to name him Alexander, yuck, sounds kinda stuffy. But he looks like a little Scooter to me, so I'm calling him Scooter."

"Scooter? Oh, my word," sighed Thelma Lou.

Outside, Bambi looked at Arty as he was forced to fight with the door to make it open. She frowned at the puddle that was collecting at his feet. "I guess that's an improvement. Come show me these babies. I hope those aren't the new cowboy boots I bought on Rodeo Drive for your birthday."

"Yes, Mama. They are." Arty squirmed in discomfort.

"They're ruined," Bambi moaned.

They walked into the hospital. Arty was dripping muddy water everywhere. It flowed behind him like a leaking drain.

Bambi entered the waiting room dramatically. She charged past the people and the nurse's station straight to the electric doors. She demanded attention, and she got it from everyone in the room.

"Arty, let me see my grandbabies. Oh, my goodness, I'm way too young to be a grandmother," she emoted, playing to the crowd like a star actress.

Nurse Feelgoode tried to cut her off. "You'll have to sign in." Suddenly Nurse Feelgoode recognized who Bambi was and almost fainted with excitement. Her face lit up with joy, "Oh, my goodness, you're Bambi Wood!"

Bambi was so pleased by the recognition, but she played the star and pushed right past her. "No autographs, please." Then she smiled and very kindly assured the nurse, "Well, maybe later."

The electric doors opened as she and Arty lunged through them. The star was gone and everyone in the waiting room was dumbstruck in wonder. Nurse Feelgoode slipped on the puddle Arty had left behind.

An old woman proudly told an old man with a walker. "I was in high school with that woman."

The old man looked at her in total disbelief. "No way. You're 96 years old."

"Exactly." The old woman answered.

Bambi and Arty made it down the empty, tile green hallway, quickly peering into each room. Arty grabbed a towel from a cleaning cart and wiped his face and hair.

"Which room is she in?" Bambi asked.

"I have no idea," Arty answered, "I never made it inside here."

Finally, she saw Thelma Lou and Grandpa hovering over Doreen's bed, admiring the babies.

"It's this one; I see her family," she told Arty, who was finishing with the towel and placed the dirty wet thing back on the cleaning woman's cart.

Bambi burst into Doreen's room, pushed Doreen's family aside, and made her grand entrance.

"Out of my way, let me see these strange baaaa..." She stuttered and stopped as all attention was turned towards her. She eyed the babies like a cobra eyeing its prey, then theatrically swooned falling to the floor. Grandpa and Thelma Lou rushed to help her.

"Mama, are you alright?"

Thelma Lou calmed Arty. "It's okay. She'll get over it. I almost fainted too."

Grandpa then helped lift Bambi up as she started to come back to her usual self.

Doreen leaned over the side of the bed watching it all as she held both babies tightly in her arms. Bambi came to and looked at Arty as he and Grandpa helped steady her on her feet.

She grabbed Arty by the arm dramatically, spun him around, and pulled him out the door. "We'll be back," she snapped before Doreen could say a word. Doreen was not happy. Bambi pulled Arty into the hospital hallway. She still had not recovered from the shock. She ushered Arty down the hallway towards the cafeteria.

"Son, your wife has either been seduced by an alien, or she is one. Either way, we're in big trouble. This better not hit the news."

"Mama, you've gone crazy."

"Get me a drink. I need a drink."

"There are coffee machines right down there in the cafeteria."

"Oh, my sweet Arty." She emotionally grabbed him and gave him a hug. Then her eyes widened in horror as she realized what she had done. She pulled away and looked down at her dress, now covered in muddy water.

"I knew it—ruined," she sobbed. "My dress—your boots—and the only place to shop in this town is Pete's Hardware."

Inside Doreen's room, Thelma Lou was talking baby talk to the twins. Doreen seemed angry. "Doesn't that just beat all? Bambi was only in here for two seconds before she grabbed Arty and hauled him out of here. She hardly even looked at the babies."

"Oh, she got a good look at the babies alright." Thelma Lou assured her.

"I wonder what she's saying to Arty. I bet it's something bad about me and the babies. She didn't want Arty to marry me."

"Oh, I wouldn't worry about her. Arty loves you."

Grandpa was looking out the window at the scrawny bushes next to the building surrounded by weeds. He turned to Thelma Lou and signed about them. Thelma Lou walked over and looked out the window too.

"Oh, what sad azaleas. They're almost dead. You're right; they do need watering."

"Why are you two worrying about some old dead bushes outside the dadblam window? Don't you want to hold Scooter, Mama?"

"Oh, yes indeed."

Arty continued to lead his mom towards the door to the coffee machines. Unfortunately, the food area was closed and dark, so Bambi and Arty surveyed the vending machines searching for hot coffee.

"Son, your wife must have been seduced by a blue alien. Weird things have happened in this town before."

Bambi found the coffee machine. She did not bother with money. She shot a few sparks from her fingers, the cup dropped, and coffee started pouring. No problem. Bambi took her coffee and looked for the sugar.

Arty, money in hand, decided to put it away and try what his mother had just done. He shot sparks from his fingers, the machine rumbled–stopped–He waited; Finally, one cup fell, and coffee started pouring. He was very pleased with himself.

"Arty, you cannot run away from the truth. Those babies just don't look normal."

"You telling me that my wife made whoopee with a little blue man is normal."

"I don't know how big he was."

At the machine, Arty took his coffee and another cup fell and started to fill.

Arty frowned and took the second cup of coffee and a third cup fell and started to fill. He sat one of the cups on a nearby table, then rushed back to grab the third cup. He turned and handed his mother the third cup; now, she had two cups.

She frowned. Another cup fell. They both sighed. Arty looked desperate.

Bambi looked at him and shook her head. "Control. It's all about control," She touched the coffee machine and it stopped pouring. "There. See?"

He set the extra coffees on the table while she went to a machine with cakes and cookies inside. Sparks flew from her finger and the machine gave her a cupcake package.

"You think this is all my fault?" Arty asked.

She handed him one of the cupcakes. "No, honey, if it were your fault, the babies would be green."

He shook his head no to the cupcake. "You eat it. I want those powdered sugar donuts. Green?" He shot the machine and the donuts fell. He felt proud of himself.

"Your father was a nature boy," she told him with a wink.

Then another package of donuts fell. "So, huh? Green?" He staggered away in a daze. They sat at a table. A few moments passed. "Green, Huh?"

"Well, greenish." Bambi demurred. "After all, our last name is Wood."

"You never talked about our father, Mama."

"You were a child. You wouldn't have understood."

Behind him, Nurse Feelgoode entered. She went to the coffee machine, put money in, and pressed the button without looking over at them.

"You think I understand now?" Arty shook his head, more confused than ever as he looked towards the malfunctioning coffee machine.

Coffee shot across the room. Cups kept falling and falling. Then the cake machine next to Nurse Feelgoode exploded sending cakes, chips, and cookies flying. She shook her head, "Another Friday night at the ER.' Then she walked out with nothing.

"What can I tell you, darling? People sometimes are not what they seem. Life is more complicated than in your simple world." Bambi made a disgusted face at her coffee and quickly watered a plant with it. "This coffee sucks." The plant immediately withered and died.

Chapter 5

Brotherly Love

V ictor and Winebombs exited a military plane at the small rundown airport of Rainbow City. A soldier greeted them with a salute. They saluted him back.

"Follow me." The soldier instructed. He walked them across the tarmac to a taco food truck with the name Pepe & Maria's painted on the side, along with a menu. The soldier pointed to the truck. "Your ride as ordered, sir." He announced.

Victor was surprised. "A taco truck?" He asked Winebombs.

"You said total concealment," she explained. "No one will suspect us in this." She spat her old bubble gum out on the pavement and popped a new piece into her mouth.

Victor was repulsed.

"The flavor's gone in this one," she insisted. "I hate it when the flavor is gone. Like chewing rubber."

"You've got to be kidding," he smirked.

The soldier walked back to his jeep and suddenly realized something was making his shoe stick to the ground. He lifted his foot, and a long thread of pink bubble gum pulled from the asphalt to the bottom of his shiny black dress shoe. It was the wad of gum Winebombs had spat on the ground which he had stepped on. He made a disgusting face, scraped the gum off on the sidewalk, got into his jeep, and drove away.

"You did that on purpose, didn't you?" Victor teased Winebombs.

"Did what?" she replied, being coy and acting innocent.

"The gum."

She smiled. "Well, there was about a fifty-fifty chance that I would spit it in the exact correct spot so he would step on it" She replied. "I calculated his rhythm and steps and spit as accurately as I thought possible."

"You are evil," he smirked.

"A girl has gotta have some fun."

They climbed into the taco truck and looked around. "Does this margarita machine really work?" Victor asked as he looked the kitchen over.

"It all works. The stove, the grill, and all the ingredients for everything on the menu. It's a perfect decoy to hide our real agenda." Winebombs explained, very pleased with herself for thinking of it. She turned a cabinet of food items around and revealed a set of screens, a computer, and a complete military arsenal.

Victor was not impressed. "How old is this equipment?" he asked as he examined the dated computer system. He turned it on and waited as it took a while to warm up and get going. "Stone Age, I see," he stated flatly, not amused.

Winebombs tried to explain. "Congressional budget cuts, sir."

"What a dump," Victor announced.

Winebombs thought he was again playing their game. She was excited and happy that she knew the answer to one. "Bette Davis? I forgot the movie."

"So has everyone else. Close. But no cigar. Google it."

She grabbed her cell phone.

In the cafeteria, Arty and Bambi sat at a table eating more junk food and drinking root beer instead of coffee.

Arty's cell phone rang. It was Doreen. Arty started to answer it, then Bambi quickly took the phone and refused the call.

"Are we going to sit here all night?" Arty asked.

"At least until we figure out what to do next. I can't face your wife."

Arty was down in the dumps. He put his face in his hands but tried to make his mom understand. "None of this is my fault."

She felt sorry for him. "I know, sweetheart. You were always the good one."

"Not always." Arty insisted. "I remember one time when I almost killed Victor.

"You tried to kill Victor?"

"I was still a baby; I didn't know what I was doing. We were crawling on the floor dressed in cute little matching outfits. Victor hated it when you dressed us the same. He always thought he was better than me. Anyway, he crawled over to Grandma's old floor lamp. He pulled the cord so hard that the metal plate fell and exposed the wires. I crawled over to see what he was looking at, and Victor grabbed my hand and stuck my finger in the socket. Electricity shocked my whole body. I sizzled for the first time. Happens all the time now, no big deal, but then it was a new experience. Victor, of course, doubled over laughing. Some brother! I think it was him laughing that made me so mad. I grabbed his hand and wouldn't let go. Then, both of us sizzled and I was the one laughing. Victor got so mad that he suddenly turned into a snake. I dropped him and he slithered away. I thought I'd killed him."

"Oh, baby. He didn't die. He's a shapeshifter like his father. You just forced him to shift."

Arty pushed her away. "Shapeshifter? I felt so bad about what I did to him that I made a promise to myself that I would never hurt another living creature ever again. And I haven't broken that promise. Where is Victor now, Mama? Where is he now?" Arty ran out of the cafeteria.

In the parking lot, he passed the taco truck which was parked with Victor and Winebombs inside. Arty did not realize his brother was sitting right there. He continued across the street and into a bar.

Two bug size metal drones flew out of the truck and followed Arty to the bar. Victor stood holding an empty metal box and a receiver. "Operation Pandora launch successful."

Winebombs called Victor over as she spied on Arty on the monitors while he ordered a drink. Then, Bambi ran across the screen and followed Arty into the bar.

"Mama?" Victor exclaimed, surprised to see her on the monitors.

"That's your mother? Bambi Wood is your mother?"

Outside Doreen's room, the dying bushes mysteriously began to grow healthier and bigger.

The limbs started to reach up and up until they were above the window. Zordak's face made of green leaves formed, and he looked through the panes of glass at the newborn babies. Willow and Scooter looked over at him and smiled. His magic continued to make the flowers bloom. Zordak's attention was drawn away as a police car pulled into the parking lot. He quickly sank back into the ground, but the bushes remained vibrantly alive and filled with beautiful pink blossoms.

The police car pulled up to the taco truck. Two cops got out and walked over to it.

Barney Landry, a middle-aged hulk of a guy with a flattop haircut, took off his cop cap and wiped the sweat from his head with a dirty, once-white handkerchief. He plopped the cap back on his fat head then banged on the window of the taco truck.

Beauregard Dingledorper. a younger cop was tall and good-looking, and he knew it. He swaggered over and read the menu. As soon as he opened his mouth his stupidity ruined all of his homeboy charm. The father of Sally Ann Dingledorper, his little tap-dancing beauty queen was the joy of his life and also the biggest pain in the butt. He had no idea she was currently in the emergency room at the hospital causing trouble.

Inside the truck, Victor and Winebombs panicked as they saw the cops on one of their screens. They jumped into action reacting to Barney's loud knocking.

Winebombs reached for her gun. "Holy snot! Good ol' boys. Should I liquidate them?"

"Breathe, Winebombs, I'll handle this," Victor whispered as he walked over to the taco truck's sliding window just as Barney banged again. Victor rolled up the window and looked out at the cops.

"Si, senores. Como estas?" Victor responded to them with a bad accent.

Barney barked his order in English. "A pork burrito, no beans, and a large margarita, no salt." He turned to his sidekick and asked, "Whatta you having Dingledorper?"

Beauregard scratched himself and thought real hard. It was so difficult for him to make any decision. He had to really think about it. When he finally spoke, his southern drawl was slower than his brain. "Well, let me see now, uh well, may I please have me...uh... that two beef taco special with rice and beans, one of them there corn dogs and a root beer float with whipped cream and a cherry on top? I loves me a cherry."

Victor rolled his eyes as he turned and looked at Winebombs, who had quickly closed the panel where the secret equipment was hidden. She jumped up, turned on the stove, and started cooking.

Chapter 6

Pickle and Dickle

B ambi recoiled from the smell as she entered the Pickle & Dickle Sports Bar. It was a joint that had seen better days and needed a good hosing down and fumigating. It smelled like dirty tennis shoes, rancid beer, and lots of good ol' boy sweat.

She spotted Arty at the bar where a bartender was serving him a beer in a cold mug. Arty sipped the beer but wanted to down it. He knew his mom had entered; he could see her in the mirror behind the bar. Bambi went over to him. The bartender was the over-chummy type, a hairy bear in a tank top that read, I'm Dickle.

"Howdy, ma'am, be right with ya." He drawled as he put Arty's cash in the register.

Bambi looked around the joint. It was empty except for two guys shooting pool in the back room near the restrooms.

Old-fashioned Christmas tree lights were strung around the place for no real reason but to be pretty. There were many different beer signs, pictures of horses, and paintings of tractors. Many sports figures' photos lined the walls, especially Saint's players, both from years past and present.

Bambi put her arm around Arty. "Darling,"— she started, but he cut her off, pulled away, and walked to a table.

"Go away, Mama. I need some time alone to think."

"And get drunk? What you need to do is get a grip on this situation, buster."

She turned to the bartender and ordered. "Beefeater martini, up, shaken, not stirred, with three olives."

The bartender looked at her like she was nuts. "Where ya think yer at, lady? A Holiday Inn?"

She shook her head in disbelief and changed her order quickly. "Straight gin, clean glass, please—make it a double—and start a tab." She went and sat at the table with Arty.

"You've lied to me all my life Mama."

"Only to protect you from the truth. You're a father now, bite the bullet and take charge of this situation."

"You told me my daddy was Elvis."

"I wish."

"Now, you're saying my daddy was green. And you don't mean a Green Bay Packer, right?"

Bambi avoided Arty's questions, "Uh...Here's your phone you left in the cafeteria. Doreen keeps calling."

Arty took the phone and looked at it as it continued ringing. "What do I tell her?"

"Tell her you can't talk right now."

"You tell her."

The bartender brought her drink over and sat it in front of her. "Here's the drink for the little lady. My name's Dickle, when ya need another round, just whistle."

The phone continued ringing.

"Where's Pickle?" she asked, being a smarty pants because she had read the sign and thought Pickle must be the other owner.

"He's over yonder sleeping," Dickle drawled as he pointed to a sleeping hound dog in a doghouse with the name "Pickle" painted on it.

Bambi rolled her eyes and downed her drink. "Make it another double, please."

"Yes, ma'am," Dickle took her glass and went back to the bar.

"Maybe some ice this time would be nice," she told him.

Arty was still looking at the ringing phone as if it were a flapping fish on the dock. "Should I pick it up, Mama?"

Outside in the parking lot, the two cops, Barney and Beauregard, were chomping down on their food like two Beavers building a dam.

Inside the taco truck, Winebombs was busy cleaning the grill. Victor opened another metal box, and a horde of mechanical insect drones flew out and across the parking lot towards the hospital.

"Dadgum, them is the biggest skeeters I ever seen," Beauregard said, amazed as the drones flew over their car. "I wouldn't wanna get bit by one of them suckers." He noisily sucked down the last of his root beer float. Then drove to the other side of the parking lot, near the front of the hospital entrance.

Victor watched the cops drive off as he turned to Winebombs and told her, "Leave that. We've got to snatch those two babies and their mother, while my brother and Mama are in that bar." He posted a closed sign on the outside of the glass and shut it.

Winebombs went back to the panel of monitors. Doreen's room popped up with a drone view from outside her room's window. Doreen, the twins, Thelma Lou and Grandpa, were seen on the screen.

Winebombs reacted and informed Victor. "There are two other people in there with her."

"Probably her family. We better call for backup. We're going to need Doctor Bobo to go in with you. They will recognize me. I look too much like my brother."

"You're so much better looking than he is."

"I always thought so myself."

"He looks like a dirty farmer."

"He is."

Suddenly there was a lot of commotion outside. Victor reopened the window slightly and peered out.

Media vans arrived in droves in the parking lot, followed by pickup trucks and cars. Soon the lot was full of people. It was a mob.

Victor panicked, slammed the window shut, and locked it. He turned to Winebombs, his face filled with fear, and shouted, "Get this truck out of here before they all want food!"

Chapter 7

Meet the Press

S ally Ann stood inside the hospital holding her cell phone, smiling as the mob descended into the waiting room. She led them to the babies.

"Them alien babies are down this way. Follow me. I'll show you." Sally Ann shouted.

They did follow her. A mass of reporters and photographers charged into Doreen's room and overwhelmed the family. Doreen was still on the phone trying to reach Arty. "Where can he be? Why isn't he answering?" She kicked at one of the intruders which caused her to drop the phone.

Inside the Pickle & Dickle Bar, Arty could not stand it another minute. "I have to answer it, Mama." He spoke into the phone. "Hello, Doreen? Doreen? There's no one there."

Bambi looked up and saw the television over the bar as the news flashed across the screen.

"Oh, my god. The media are here." she motioned for Arty to look at the television.

The current scene in Doreen's room flashed across the screen in the bar. It was a circus. Thelma Lou beat several reporters with her purse. Doreen's military training kicked in with a karate chop that sent a reporter hurling across the room.

Nurse Feelgoode in total shock, stood holding the twins as a caption on the screen read, *Mom Births Aliens in Louisiana!*

Bambi jumped out of her seat in the bar and pointed at the television. "We are in trouble—worldwide news. We've got to get back to help Doreen."

Arty looked up at the screen. His mouth was hanging open in total amazement at what he was witnessing. "Doreen is a TV star." he shouted, "She has a black belt in karate, you know. Did you see that guy fly across the room? That's my gal."

"It's not Doreen the world is looking at, it's your turquoise children."

Arty put his face in his hands in despair. "You know I hate dealing with the press; they make my feet sweat. I can't do any interviews."

"Get up, Arty. Be a man."

Suddenly a herd of press reporters rushed into the bar. "Where's the father?" They demanded to know from the bartender. He was more confused than they were. He had no idea.

Bambi grabbed Arty, pulled him up and pushed him towards the back. "Get up Arty, head to the restroom or daddy is going to make his television debut right now."

"I'm still dirty from the mud." he reminded her. "And I smell like horse sweat from Mister Jasper."

They ran to the back, past the two guys playing pool. Bambi pushed Arty into the ladies' room. "Quick, hide in here," she told him as she rushed up to the two pool players and zapped them with a bolt of her special energy. "You didn't see anybody, and you don't know anything. Go in the men's room and take your clothes off to cause a distraction." She commanded them.

They became like zombies controlled by her force. They repeated together. "We didn't see anybody, and we don't know anything." She zapped them again. "We're gonna go into the men's room and take our clothes off to create a distraction." They went into the men's room. Bambi rushed into the ladies' room.

The herd of press reporters raced into the men's room looking for Arty. Lots of noise, yelling, and screaming could be heard before they rushed out again.

"Those dudes are almost naked," one reporter chortled to another. "You think maybe they are aliens?"

Bambi locked the ladies' room door. She pushed Arty toward the stalls and followed him. "Third stall in the back. Jump up on the toilet. Squat. Trust me; I've done this before."

They went into the same toilet stall together. Arty jumped up on the seat and squatted, so his feet could not be seen. Bambi stood in front of him, so her feet did show.

The press banged on the door until they finally burst through and entered the ladies' room. The men looked around under the stalls. "He's not in here," One called to the other.

"There's a woman's feet in that stall." the other one confirmed.

"Well, it is the ladies' room after all." the other reporter replied as he rolled his eyes.

Bambi shouted from inside the stall, "Can't a girl have some privacy—perverts! You should be arrested."

They reacted to her voice, realized they were men in a ladies' room, panicked and rushed out.

Bambi turned to her son and motioned to him. "Quick, crawl out the window into that dumpster."

"Dumpster?" Arty was confused as he stood on the seat and turned to the window.

"You can't get any dirtier."

He struggled to get the window open. "What about my father? Who is he?" Arty asked as he finally got the window to go up.

Bambi replied as she pushed him up, "He's not from around here."

Arty climbed out, but it was a tight fit. He lost his balance and fell from the window into a large dumpster full of garbage bags. Bambi stepped onto the toilet like a pro, pulled herself up and out the window with ease. Arty landed face down in the garbage bags. Bambi fell in behind him.

"Your father is a creature of nature, he's probably somewhere out in the woods."

"You mean he camps out in the woods like a hobo?" Arty asked as he stood up and jumped out of the dumpster onto the pavement.

"He's not a hobo," Bambi assured him as she landed right by his side.

At the front door of the hospital, Barney the cop was trying to control the press who was charging through the parking lot.

Beauregard, his sidekick, seemed more interested in being on camera. "I seen them babies when they brought 'em in." He bragged to a cameraman as a female announcer held a mic in his face.

"Did you know they were aliens?" The female announcer asked him.

Beauregard had to scratch himself and think for a while before answering her. "Well, I ain't seen no spaceships around, so I thought maybe they was Smurfs."

Barney hissed at him. "Shut up, Beauregard, and help get these barricades up. Gotta get this crowd back, it has gotten out of control here."

Beauregard jumped to it, but he was disappointed. The cameraman turned off his light and the female announcer shrugged. They walked away.

"Dadblamcit, I mighta been discovered. I wanna be a TV star. I got the looks." He told Barney.

The two cops tried to get the crowd out of the hospital and back into the parking lot. Sally Ann saw Beauregard and panicked. "Oh gosh, Daddy can't find me here," she exclaimed out loud. She pushed her baby buggy through the people, down the hallway in the opposite direction.

As she did, she saw Nurse Feelgoode exit Doreen's room with the turquoise twins in a hospital cart. A young doctor instructed her. "Get those babies down to the nursery and guard them. We must keep them safe. We need to calm down the mother."

Behind him, Doreen stood on her bed screaming. "Where is Arty? Will someone go find my husband!"

Inside the taco truck, Victor and Winebombs were also in a panic.

"This is terrible. The press is everywhere." Victor moaned.

"So much for containment," Winebombs added.

Victor turned to her with instructions. "Call for help right now. We need to dump this taco truck and replace it with a television camera crew van. Then, we'll fit in with this mob."

Winebombs rushed to her computer and started typing. "I'm right on it, sir."

"How am I going to get to those babies now?" he pondered aloud.

"This is all Dana's fault. She made us late."

Victor got an idea. He paced, then turned to Winebombs and told her, "We need Dana and Doctor Bobo too. That's it. Change of plans. Call them all."

"They are all already on their way." she smiled to herself, proud that she had already called them.

Inside Doreen's room, the doctor was helping Doreen to calm down and lay back in her bed when Thelma Lou looked towards the window and shrieked.

"What is it now, Mother?"

"Those dying azaleas are now in full bloom!"

Chapter 8

The Performance

In her room, Doreen watched the news with her mother. Arty entered with Bambi. "We're worldwide news," he announced as if they didn't already know.

"Arty, where have you been?" Doreen was miffed. She couldn't believe that Arty had been out running around who knows where while she had to fend off the invaders. "I could have really used your help when we were attacked by all those press people. You are a daddy now. I need you. Your babies need you."

"I'm sorry honey but it wasn't my fault. Hey, I saw you throw that guy across the room. I was so proud of you." Arty recounted Doreen's heroic karate move. Doreen couldn't suppress a proud smile when she thought of the satisfaction she got when that pipsqueak freaked out and ran away.

"That was a pretty awesome move if I do say so myself." As usual, Doreen was starting to thaw under Arty's adoring gaze. She threw Arty a kiss.

"What is that foul odor?" Thelma Lou asked. She wrinkled her nose with a disgusted look on her face. "Smells like a dumpster."

"Was," Bambi replied.

Thelma Lou walked over to Arty and shook his hand. "I owe you an apology young man. I underestimated your abilities. Doreen was just telling us how courageous you were delivering the babies all by yourself out there in that barn."

"We were surrounded by cows, but they didn't help much," Doreen added. "Except for the one cow that fixed the hay so I could be more comfortable."

Arty felt bashful from all of the attention. "Aw, there wasn't anything to it. Once Doreen told me to catch 'em like a football, heck I made two touchdowns in one play."

"You're my hero." Doreen hugged him again and kissed him on the cheek.

There was a knock on the door. Doctor Bobo entered with Nurse Winebombs. They were both disguised in bad wigs. Doctor Bobo wore green scrubs that were too small for him. He had on big glasses and a fake nose. A weird-looking stethoscope from a child's toy box hung around his neck.

Winebombs was decked out in a fully decorated military dress uniform from a bygone era. On her head, she wore an ill-fitting nurse's cap that looked like something from a World War Two battlefield. She resembled a nurse from a comedy sketch on Saturday Night Live.

"Good evening. We've been called by the authorities to examine the, uh, bluish twins." Doctor Bobo addressed them ceremoniously.

"Turquoise." Doreen corrected him in a low, tired voice.

"What authorities?" Thelma Lou demanded to know.

"Uh...the authorities who are in authority," he told her. I've been sent to access and assist you in your current situation."

"We're accessing and assisting," Nurse Winebombs added for no good reason. Doctor Bobo gave her a strange look. If looks could kill, she would have been dead.

The taco van, now parked down the street in an area full of bushes, was completely hidden from view. Victor sat watching the screen monitoring the action in Doreen's room. He shook his head as he buried his face in his hands. He couldn't believe the stupidity of the charade playing out in the hospital room.

"I'm Doctor Bobo of the famous Bobos of Spain. And this is Nurse Winebombs, formerly of the Pensacola Naval Base military hospital.

"He's a specialist. I nurse sailors." She snapped to attention and saluted.

"What kind of specialist?" Arty asked.

"I'm a skin-tone analogist." Doctor Bobo lied, making his story up as he went along.

"A blue baby doctor," Nurse Winebombs threw in for good measure.

"They're turquoise," Doreen told her sharply.

"Turquoise, aqua, cobalt blue, what's the difference? They are not normal, kiddo." Winebombs cackled.

Doctor Bobo quickly cut her off, with another killer look. He had just committed murder twice in his mind. "That will be all Nurse—I'm the doctor. Please wait outside."

"I thought I was gonna get to draw blood," she whined.

"Oh yes, of course. Please prepare the medical cart while I update the family on their precious babies," he commanded, as he pushed her towards the door. He whispered in her ear. "Find the babies, they are probably resting in the nursery."

"Aye, aye captain," Winebombs clicked her heels and gave an exaggerated salute.

"Ahhhh yes, well, ...uh yes, ...well ok," Doctor Bobo stuttered as he awkwardly returned her salute.

Bobo turned on all of his limited charm for the family. He knew things were going badly. He had never been in a play-acting situation like this before. He had always spent all of his time working alone with patients in the lab. Bobo was extremely uncomfortable in his new role.

"Well now, I'm here to assure you that your babies are strong and healthy," he stated with a totally fabricated confidence. "They are completely normal." He chuckled nervously as he searched for more phony explanations. "That is except perhaps for the fact that the children, well...uh...children unexplainably...uh...uh..."

Doreen had heard enough, "Will you spit it out and stop wastin' my time."

"Skin color—well in the blue palette—so now we will be taking the infants to our specialized laboratory for experimentation."

Everybody in the room let out a collective gasp of horror.

In the van, Victor pounded his fists on the console and shouted, "You idiot, you imbecile, you method actor." No one heard him.

Quickly Doctor Bobo tried to cover up the mistake he made by telling the truth...Uh... I mean a medical facility to examine them and test them thoroughly.

"No way are you getting your hands on my babies, and they are turquoise, not blue." Doreen countered, her anger building into a hormonal rage.

"Turquoise is a shade of blue." Doctor Bobo defended his comment.

"I said, they are *not* blue," Doreen growled. Steam was almost coming out of her ears.

Doctor Bobo was shocked and trembled. He had never seen a woman in this state unless she was hooked up to one of his machines.

"Well, of course, if you say so, after all, you are the mother," he giggled nervously. "Maybe you should participate in the medical exam at the laboratory yourself."

Thelma Lou, Bambi and Doreen all bristled at once.

Suddenly Nurse Winebombs entered, pushing a cart. As she passed by him, she whispered to Doctor Bobo. "The little monsters are asleep in the nursery."

"Perfect," Bobo responded, relieved to be rescued from his uncomfortable acting job and Doreen's outburst. "Please start with the mother, ladies first." Bobo cheerfully instructed her.

"You betcha." Winebombs pulled out a syringe with a large needle and jabbed Doreen.

"Ouch, You're a vampire."

"I've been called that before."

"How much blood do you need?"

"Relax, I'm gonna need more from the father. It's probably his fault."

Arty recoiled, remembering his recent conversation with Bambi about his greenish daddy.

He responded with an uncomfortable laugh. "You think it's my fault—I don't think it's my fault—is it my fault?" He looked around the room for support.

"Dang Arty, ignore that stuff, they are talking about our gorgeous healthy babies like there is something wrong with them." Doreen spat out the words like a machine gun. Then she glared at Doctor Bobo with such ferocity that he seemed to wither into the corner like a faded wallflower.

Finished with her first victim, Winebombs lunged at Arty's veins with a Godzilla size needle. He recoiled in terror.

"That's a gigantic needle." Arty panicked.

"You're a big boy." She assured him, with a big smile. She was really enjoying this way too much.

Winebombs started to blow a large pink bubble from the bubble gum she was chewing, as she continued to draw Arty's blood. Winebombs' gum was getting bigger and bigger until suddenly it popped.

The sound of the bubble gum pop made everyone scream. Winebombs' face was covered in pink bubble gum. She jerked the needle out of Arty's arm.

Arty almost fainted.

Winebombs peeled the bubble gum off her face, rolled it into a ball, and popped it back into her mouth. Everyone in the room moaned in disgust.

In the hallway, Sally Ann pushed her baby buggy down the hall to the nursery. She stood on her tippy toes to look in and saw the turquoise twins along with a few other babies. Nurse Feelgoode was sitting in a chair reading a book while guarding the door. Sally Ann quickly dialed her cell phone as she picked up her inhaler. Its mist mutated into the form of Quegor as it slowly swirled into her lungs.

At the front desk, the receptionist picked up her ringing phone. Sally Ann disguised her voice at the other end of the line. "Emergency call for Nurse Feelgoode."

Sally Ann quickly hid in a broom closet and peered out. She saw the receptionist walk down the hall and tell Nurse Feelgoode about the call. Nurse Feelgoode jumped up and left with the receptionist.

Inside Doreen's room, Winebombs took vial after vial of Arty's blood. Finally, Bambi stopped her. "That's enough of my son's blood. His blood sugar is probably low," Bambi demanded being a concerned mother

"Don't worry. Grandpa went to buy donuts." Thelma Lou told her.

When donuts were mentioned, Doctor Bobo did a double-take. Bobo snapped back to the job at hand. "Nurse, time for you to take the children's blood."

Doreen objected. "Keep your hands off my babies."

"The little monsters will love it," Winebombs exclaimed. She rushed to push the cart out and then cackled.

"Don't you worry," Doctor Bobo interjected hurriedly to calm Doreen, "we won't do a thing without their guardian's permission."

Nurse Winebombs triumphantly whispered to Doctor Bobo, "Yeah, their guardian Victor Wood."

"Shush now, Winebombs, take the little needles and the small vials with you. Get the babies now and let's go—hurry," he instructed her under his breath.

She made a face and went out unhappily, still chewing her gum. "Yes, doctor," she said sarcastically, before slamming the door.

Everybody in the room reacted to the violent slamming of the door.

Sally Ann crept into the baby nursery and quickly
proceeded over to the turquoise twin's bed. She carried
her two dolls. She took the male doll as she stood
next to Scooter, and she pulled her voodoo pin out of
her hair and got ready to stab the doll. One of little
Scooter's eyes opened and he held up his tiny hand just
as Sally Ann jabbed the doll's rubber head with the pin.
Her eyes widened in the realization that her spell had
boomeranged back on her. She grabbed her head in pain
and covered her mouth to mute her scream.

Winebombs was strolling down the other hallway
towards the baby viewing area. She turned the corner
and was surprised to see Sally Ann pushing her baby
buggy down the hall in the opposite direction. When
she got to the window, Winebombs peered inside and
saw the twin's bed. She headed into the room.

At the front desk, Nurse Feelgoode spoke into the
receptionist's phone. "Hello? Hello? They must have
hung up."

Chapter 9

Box of Donuts

D octor Bobo was rattling on and on about how there were some blue people in Kentucky to which the family might be related. He was interrupted when Grandpa entered with a box of donuts. He handed them out to everyone. Bobo stood transfixed.

At that moment, Doctor Bobo seemed to forget about his assigned mission. Instead, he had more important things on his mind as he watched the box of donuts get passed around the room.

Thelma Lou bit into her donut and reacted joyfully. "Oh, goody—lemon jelly—My favorite."

At the mention of "lemon jelly," Doctor Bobo started to salivate.

In the taco truck hidden in the bushes, Victor became alarmed. He muttered out loud to himself. "You better not eat one of those donuts, Bobo!"

In the room, Grandpa signed something.

"They are all lemon jelly? How wonderful." Thelma Lou told everyone.

After passing everyone a donut, there was one left. Grandpa offered it to Doctor Bobo who reached for it hungrily, then stopped himself. It was almost as if he could hear Victor's scream in the van.

"Uh, no thanks, I'm on a diet," he lied.

"Oh, have one." Thelma Lou told him. "One jelly donut won't kill you."

As she talked with her mouth full, some of the lemon jelly started to run down her lips. She licked it back in. Doctor Bobo really wanted that last donut. He wiped the sweat from his brow with his handkerchief. He reached for the donut and stopped himself again.

Grandpa shrugged and put the box with the last donut down on the food tray near the computer. Doctor Bobo started to sweat buckets. Boy, he wanted that donut so

badly, but he knew what would happen if he ate it. He
would scare everyone and ruin Victor's plan.

In the van, Victor was screaming at the monitor as he
feared The Glob would soon destroy everything. "Don't
you dare eat that donut, Bobo."

Doctor Bobo could not stand the temptation for
another minute. He turned to grab that donut, just as
Grandpa, who had finished his first one, started to take
a bite of the last one. Bobo went berserk. In the process,
his fake nose came loose but did not fall off.

"Give me that donut," he screamed, completely out of
control now. He fought Grandpa for the last bite. But
Grandpa swallowed it down.

"Noooooooo," he screamed in complete agony as he
snatched the empty box away from Grandpa.

Everyone in the room was shocked and confused at the
outburst. Most of all, Grandpa tried to figure out what
he had done and started signing madly. Thelma Lou
could not keep up with what he was trying to say.

Suddenly, there was a commotion in the hallway. Winebombs entered with the babies hidden under a blanket on a baby hospital cart. "Come on, Bobo. I've got the babies. Let's get out of here."

Just then, Nurse Feelgoode rushed into the room. "Did a member of your family take the twins out of the nursery without checking with me?"

"What are you talking about?" Doreen demanded angrily.

Doctor Bobo was crying hysterically, holding the donut box as if it was precious gold. He licked the bottom of the empty box wildly and caused his fake nose to fall off along with his glasses.

Nurse Feelgoode noticed Doctor Bobo and Nurse Winebombs for the first time. "Who are you people?"

"What? They aren't part of the hospital staff?" Stunned, Thelma Lou flew into a panic.

Doreen yelled. "He's a fake—she's got our babies. Get her!"

They all chased Winebombs out of the room. She was completely confused about Doctor Bobo's behavior.

"Bobo, help me," she pleaded as she ran faster. She ran down one hallway and turned onto another.

In the taco truck, Victor was going berserk watching the monitor, helpless to do anything.

He barked at the screen. "Forget that stupid Glob, get those babies to me!"

He ran to the driver's seat and started the motor to the van.

Doctor Bobo ran out of Doreen's room and into the hallway. "My glasses." He was blind without them. He ran into a wall and knocked himself out cold and fell to the floor.

Winebombs turned a corner and headed down another hallway. The family and the hospital staff chased her. She ran into the cafeteria.

The coffee machine was still shooting coffee everywhere. Cups were dropping down and rolling on the floor. There were piles of cakes and potato chips and donuts spewing from that machine.

Winebombs slipped on the floor from the flood of coffee. The baby's cart went flying out of her hands and crashed into a wall with a loud bang. The cart turned over, spilling its contents onto the floor. Everyone screamed.

Arty and Doreen ran to the babies to see if they were okay. But, when they pulled the blanket off, there were no babies, only two baby dolls.

"These aren't my babies," Doreen exclaimed. "These are toy baby dolls! Oh, my lord, where are they?"

A sinister giggle was heard. Sally Ann burst out of the emergency room doors with her baby doll carriage. The turquoise babies were inside.

She headed out of the parking lot down the street onto Main Street, past the Pickle & Dickle bar and several blocks of stores.

Looming in the distance ahead of her was a giant bridge spanning the Mississippi River. It was lit by lights that showed the mighty water flowing below it.

Sally Ann did not care about the babies, she only wanted them gone so she wouldn't have to share the spotlight. "I'm throwing you little monsters into the Mighty Mississippi. There's only room for one star in this town."

She laughed out loud as she passed the taco truck hidden in the bushes. It charged out with a roar and followed her. Victor had been watching the entire series of events on his monitors.

The family was too far away in the distance but continued to chase Sally Ann.

The taco truck was right on her heels. She looked at it with puzzlement. "Where the heck did that come from?" she asked herself as she raced faster and faster. Victor gunned the motor and pushed his foot on the gas to the floorboard. He was flying. She screeched at him, "Who are you?"

Suddenly, Sally Ann came to the end of the street where there was a concrete barricade. She headed down a pedestrian sidewalk that led through the park to the edge of the river. She was scared and ran as fast as her little feet could carry her, with the tap shoes a tap tap tappin'.

She hit the dead end at the river and gleefully sent the baby carriage over the wall. The babies went flying off the cliff, through the air towards the river. Vahlmalia blew a gentle breeze from the sky to soften their landing.

Victor couldn't stop the truck and he crashed into the concrete barrier. He and the truck went flying through the air. There was a loud splash in the river.

Sally Ann ran away and hid in some bushes. She was totally stunned and out of breath. She saw the other people coming and took off in another direction.

The family and the hospital staff reached the edge of the river. They were desperately looking down at the dark water.

Bambi was furious. "Where is that little girl? I'll spank her good; somebody call the police," she snarled as she ran off in the direction Sally Ann had disappeared.

Thelma Lou ran and grabbed the chain-link fence separating them from the river and shook it violently, screaming until she was blue in the face. Doreen grabbed her mother's shoulders. "Mama—calm down—you're hysterical."

"Let me save them." Thelma Lou pleaded, bursting into tears.

"No, Mama, you know you can't help when you get like this. Let Grandpa take you home. We'll handle this. Everybody get out of the way. Go home."

"What are you going to do?" Thelma Lou whimpered.

"I'm going to climb this fence and get my babies."

"Doreen, you can't do that," Arty shouted and stopped her.

"Watch me." Doreen continued to hold onto the fence as Arty restrained her calmly.

Grandpa put his arm around Thelma Lou and led her away.

"There's nothing we can do," Feelgoode observed. "I need to get back to the hospital and attend to my patients."

Winebombs scooted down the sidewalk undetected by everybody as she desperately searched for Victor. She was unaware he went over the wall and into the water. Victor swam to shore and climbed up on the rocky embankment looking very much like a yucky green mud river monster.

Winebombs sobbed "Oh my poor, poor doctor."

Only Arty and Doreen were left at the river. "We can't give up hope yet," Doreen cried as she tugged at Arty's shirt.

Arty suddenly saw the baby carriage in the water. For some strange reason, it was not sinking below the current. "There they are!" he shouted as he pointed at the river.

"It's a miracle," Doreen gasped when she saw the baby carriage floating in the water.

Doreen, still in her hospital gown, immediately started to scale the chain-link fence again.

"Wait a minute, Doreen, you sure you want to climb the fence when you just had babies?"

"Stop wasting time, Arty, c'mon."

But Arty was frozen as he looked down the steep cliff leading to the river. He frowned and scratched his head in disbelief for a moment.

"Arty, I'm not waiting for you—come or don't—I'm going"

"Wait a minute. I don't understand why they're not floating down the river. They're floating upriver against the current."

"How is that?" Doreen asked.   "What's holding them up? Why isn't the baby carriage sinking?"

"It makes no sense. If they'd landed on a plank of wood, they'd be floating down the river." Arty answered her.

Yet, the baby carriage was slowly, steadily moving upriver. Suddenly the carriage wheels rose up out of the water as a large yellow eye emerged. Slowly the Leviathan-sized beast carrying the babies rose from the river in all his glory. The baby carriage rested on the back of a ten-foot-long alligator.

"A gator's got them. He'll eat them alive!" Doreen screamed

Arty turned to Doreen, "I know this is going to sound crazy, but I know that gator."

"You know a gator?" Doreen asked him, shocked, thinking that he had gone nuts.

Suddenly, Arty was excited and optimistic. His despair had turned to hope, a strange, hard-to-explain kind of hope, but hope all the same. "Yeah, he lives in the swamp behind our farm. Sometimes Grandpa and I go fishing there. We feed him."

"Feed him?" Doreen asked, horrified.

"Let's head home."

"Home?" She was becoming more and more confused

"That's where he's taking them. Trust me." Arty helped Doreen back over the fence.

"He's not going to eat them then?" Doreen asked.

Arty smiled and replied, "Nah, he's a vegan. I call him Zordak."

Chapter 10

Up The River

The gator continued carrying the babies up the Mississippi River. There was something uncanny about these newborns besides their turquoise coloring. Even though they had been born just a few hours ago, they seemed to have developed at an accelerated rate. Usually, a newborn's coordination is still undeveloped, and they still have not mastered their reactions to the new world around them.

The twins seemed to have an unusual sense of curiosity and a keen awareness of excitement about their environment. They had abilities that most infants wouldn't have until they were at least six months old. It held a clue to the possibilities that would unfold in the future.

One example was that the sound of a calliope gained the infant's attention. It was played by a woman in a feathered hat and a lavender antebellum dress. She sat

on the top deck of the Mississippi paddleboat Natchez
as it slowly rolled by them.

They were fascinated by the white steam that rose from
the bright silver pipes of the organ as she played an
old southern song. It was a haunting melody, extremely
hummable because of its simplicity, that brought back a
long-forgotten era in Louisiana.

In the olden days, the showboats were the floating
theaters of their time, presenting entertainment to small
towns and cities along the river. Today they were a
tourist ride that provided a slow, relaxing trip down
memory lane.

Blackish dark gray smoke rose from the two red
smokestacks beside the captain's cabin at the top level
of the boat right in front of the calliope platform. The
captain steered the boat. He was dressed just like many
captains before him in a fancy uniform from an early era.
It was once the actual uniform worn, but today it was a
costume for a show. The smiling young captain waved
to Zordak who he called Granddaddy Gator. The twins
smiled as the boat came into view.

Scooter and Willow stood on their tippy-toes and held
onto the doll carriage's side as the water gently moved
around the gator. They giggled with joy at the sight of
the activity on the riverboat. They had no idea yet it was
a show, simply an illusion put on with actors dressed as
belles and beaus in fancy dresses and old-style suits.

The tourists were the real people today in colorful shorts and tennis shoes. They busily snapped pictures of the babies with their cell phones. They thought the weird turquoise babies floating up the river were just a strange tourist gimmick. The joyful tourists on board sang happily on their way down river headed to New Orleans for a night of drinking and partying on Bourbon Street.

The innocent babies were alive and took in every sight they saw, inhaled every new smell they encountered, every sound their ears heard. They were learning lessons about their new home at a fast pace. Never underestimate the memories of a day-old child. Every second was being recorded and encoded with meaning in their quickly forming brains. They had been born with a purpose and their skin color would not be the most amazing aspect of their future.

Everything that happened to them had a special meaning. Their future adventures and achievements had been mapped out in the stars. Their destiny was unstoppable.

The colossal, red paddles rotated through the water pushing the showboat forward as they had for over a hundred and fifty years. The kids delighted in the swishing sound the water made as it flowed over the big wooden paddles before splashing back into the river.

As the paddleboat churned its way down the river out of view, the waves caused by the turning paddles created ripples that rocked the baby's carriage as it perilously was perched upon the gator. Their little hands grasped the sides of the doll wagon to keep from falling. They looked at each other and smiled, each would remember the moment they both realized one had to hold on tight to survive in this world.

The river calmed for a moment, and they relaxed, but only for a moment. No sooner had the riverboat passed out of sight, than a new, disturbing sound hurt the twin's ears. A loud horn blast announced another boat on its way, this time headed upriver like they were. The rusty orange front of a monstrous, modern oil tanker rushed by them at a swift pace. It was headed to the oil refineries in Baton Rouge.

The long boat passed by Granddaddy Gator and babies. It caused the carriage to rock from its wake which was much stronger as it passed. The babies knew to grab hold to the side and rock with the alligator. They were learning so fast. They giggled from the excitement. By this time, they had realized they could still communicate with each other as they had in their mother's womb, by just telepathic communication. Unlike most human infants they would not forget where they had come from, what their purpose was, and why they were born.

Suddenly a cluster of dragonflies circled around the kids. This was something new. Something they had not encountered before. The buzzing sound of the creature's wings as they hovered in front of the babies was astonishing. The dragonflies seemed as curious about the babies as the babies were about them. Willow squealed in delight as she realized she could understand what the beautiful creatures were saying. The twins could communicate with nature telepathically too.

The dragonflies had accomplished their mission and flew away as suddenly as they came. The babies realized you had to look quick because things moved quickly in this new world. Opportunities must be seized in the moment, or they would be gone.

The dragonflies were followed by a swarm of lovely butterflies in beautiful colors as they swirled around Granddaddy Gator and the babies in a magical dance. The kids gazed in wonder at the delicate wings and then—woosh—the butterflies were gone, too, in an instant.

Vahlmalia playfully continued to generate strong gusts of wind, helping Zordak navigate the turn around the river bend. The twins were delighted by their bumpy ride.

On the shore were wooden shacks that came right down to the river's edge. People lived in the shacks. A few folks sat on rickety wharves in folding chairs, they stared at the dark river and marveled at the size of the gator floating by with a baby carriage stuck on his back.

One fella jumped up and ran towards his shack, telling the others that he was going to get his shotgun and shoot that gator to make gumbo. The babies heard Zordak laugh to himself and tell them to hold on tight. As Granddaddy Gator, he picked up speed and swam faster.

They left that section of the river far behind before the man ever emerged from his shack. Willow and Scooter's eyes widened in realization as they looked at each other happily—they could understand and speak gator.

The waters turned a foul oily green and, on the shore, a sprawling, brightly lit chemical plant spewed toxic chemical waste through long, big rusty pipes. The waste poured into the river and created an ugly nasty color to the water and a horrible smell filled the air.

The babies made a sour face and put their little fingers to their noses. A red-hot flame of fire belched from a towering furnace and sent tall plumes of black smoke into the night sky. It was Quegor personified.

This section of the river brought hordes of buzzing, nasty flies that lived and thrived off of the toxic chemicals in the water. The disgusting, noisy flies circled around the babies but did not bite them.

Scooter swatted at the flies with one hand while still holding on with the other. He realized the flies had a place on earth and were created by the same life force as he was. Both kids were glad to get away from this section of the river as soon as possible. They also realized that cleaning up foul places like this on earth was an important part of their mission.

Many more ugly chemical plants poured rancid smoke into the air. They stood in a seemingly unending procession along the river. What was once a beautiful old southern mansion sat on the riverfront. It was now dark and deserted, rotting and falling down. Its majestic once-white columns are blackened by the soot of the smokestacks. People could no longer live or survive here. However, many still tried.

An old, crumbling sign on the shore nailed onto a rotting board, obviously left by a protester many years ago, read Cancer Alley. A skeleton face with crossbones made Willow wince in disgust. She knew in her heart that this was not a nice place. Nature was dying here, as the trees were leafless and barren, only weeds survived.

The gator swam on the river more quickly trying to escape the horror of the ugly mess around them. Scooter and Willow had gotten their first lesson in how man was destroying himself with pollution and greed. They could smell the rot and saw the ruins of a once beautiful shoreline and they would never forget it. The stench had made an indelible impression on their minds.

Soon the shore turned beautiful again. A forest of lovely green cypress trees with gray moss hanging from their limbs came into view against the now-clear night sky. They gazed at the stars twinkling above and a slow-moving white cloud moved across the glow of a crescent moon hanging over their heads.

Bushes of blooming flowers were everywhere now. Wild honeysuckle filled the air with a wonderful, sweet smell.

Scooter sighed with relief as he sniffed wild magnolia blossoms on stately tall trees. Willow marveled at the sight of many beautifully colored birds chirping their sweet song in the limbs of the trees. In the east, the red dawn of an early morning sun started its slow steady rise on the horizon as the moon descended. It was a magic time for the twins. Their first experience of the change from night into day.

The weary gator, tired from his long, difficult swim against the red river's current slowly turned into a small creek that flowed lazily into the Mississippi. The bayou was the lovely, serene habitat of many of Louisiana's creatures. Granddaddy Gator was almost home, and it revived his spirit and renewed his strength to be in the slow-moving water of the swamp that would twist and turn until it reached the family farm.

A pelican swooped down and caught a catfish in its beak, then flew off. Little fish jumped higher and higher to get a quick glimpse of the turquoise twins as they passed by. Every creature in the swamp knew that the twins had been sent to earth to help nature recover. Scooter and Willow gurgled in delight as they communicated with the fish. They marveled at the wonders around them. They were delighted to see all this nature thriving with abundance for the first time in their lives.

As the merriment wound down, they grew drowsy and laid down in the carriage and rested as the gator swam up close to the shore. The water of the swamp was slow and peaceful. The babies yawned, stretched their little arms, and held onto each other as they fell asleep.

After a while, the shadows of the cypress trees hanging with moss overhead passed away. They were replaced with a bank filled with tall grasses, weeds, and big weeping willow trees. The gator saw a silhouette of Arty and Doreen who stood on a clearing of grass nearby. The gator got close enough for Arty to grab the doll carriage. He lifted it in the air and set it on dry land.

"It's great to have friends in the animal kingdom. Thanks, Zordak."

The happy Alligator rolled over several times to acknowledge Arty's thank you, disappeared under the water's depths, and was gone to take his morning nap. Arty had no idea who Zordak really was or why he had befriended Arty and Grandpa in the first place. Some things are best kept secret until the right time to be revealed.

Doreen took the twins out of the baby doll carriage and hugged each one gently. Scooter yawned and fell right back to sleep. Willow was awake and excited. She touched her mama's cheek with her little hand and looked deep into her mama's eyes. Oh, how she was yearning to tell her parents about all the wonders she had seen and experienced on the trip up the river. But, alas, she had not learned to speak yet, so she could only express herself through her eyes. Doreen stared into her baby girl's eyes and understood.

"Oh, my little soldiers, you already had your first adventure, didn't you?"

Willow giggled.

Doreen held them both close as they walked to the old pickup truck sitting a few feet away. Arty threw Sally Ann's baby carriage into the back of the truck.

The sun was steadily rising over the swamp as the family got in their truck and headed across a field towards home.

Chapter 11

The Dream

Thelma Lou woke up suddenly, startled from her deep sleep. "That dream again. Why do I keep having the same dream? A waterfall—a man—out of nowhere. Did he come from the sea? I can't remember the rest. Did that really happen to me? Was it in California?—Hawaii?—North Carolina? Could he be Doreen's father?" she uttered out loud without realizing it. Thelma Lou lay flailing in her bed, but she couldn't get her mind to settle down.

As she struggled, she realized the sun was rising outside of her window, but it was still dark in her room. She reached over to turn on the bedside lamp and knocked over the wig stand holding her curly poodle wig; the wig that she hid behind in her daily public life. "Stupid wig," she exclaimed, and the memory of the man in her dream vanished.

She leaned over to pick the wig up from the floor, her beautiful thick long hair draped across her face. She was surprisingly beautiful in the morning light that began to pour in through the window.

She held the ugly wig in one hand and used the other to sweep the hair out of her face. She laid back on her pillow staring up at the ceiling still holding the wig as memories of the past flooded into her consciousness.

She began to beat herself up. "I had no strength of character, I'm just a useless pile of emotional jelly unable to act when it really mattered" She pounded her pillow in frustration. Then realized she had messed up her wig, which she put back on the stand.

"Why was I so useless when those precious babies needed me to save them? I watched as they disappeared upriver. Useless, just useless, same as when my mother was dying, useless when my brother was killed overseas. Why couldn't I use the abilities I was given to save them, instead I'm just an emotional mess."

Once again, she involuntarily jerked her arm and knocked the wig stand over again. This time she picked it up and flung it across the room as angry tears stung her eyes. What good was her intelligence, creativity, and personal power when she posed in her daily life as a nervous, empty-headed poodle?

She laid back resigned as she masked her anger just like she always did, not only from others but from herself. She had learned from the nuns that educated her after her mother passed when she was five. All of the magic her mother had encouraged in her was a recipe for getting her knuckles whacked by a ruler. She had to hide who she was at all costs.

When Grandpa returned from the Middle East, he revived the rundown family farm. She came home from the convent. Here, in this small town, she learned that a powerful female was shunned when she revealed her true self to this community. So, she created the silly non-threatening version of Thelma Lou that fit in nicely with the local culture.

There were only a handful of occasions when she revealed herself to the world. As she remembered those moments, she felt a rush of relief from worrying about Doreen and her babies.

She wandered mentally back to January nineteen seventy when she was nineteen years old and came face to face with the truest version of herself.

She overheard a coworker raving about some bands that were playing at the Warehouse in New Orleans, only a bus ride away. So, she took a chance and went to hear Fleetwood Mac and the Grateful Dead. Her friend introduced Thelma Lou to the bands' members. Thelma

Lou had connected to her tribe. From the first note, she knew something special was going to happen for her.

Thelma Lou went home and told Grandpa that she planned to travel with the Grateful Dead and wanted to know if he was going to be alright

"But I heard the band was arrested," Grandpa's hands flew as he signed, and his face filled with concern.

"The cops framed the band and arrested me and my friends, it was so exciting."

Grandpa realized it was time for him to let her go and follow her destiny.

To her surprise, Grandpa pulled some money he had been saving out of the bottom of the refrigerator and gave it to her. She packed a few clothes, some of her arts and crafts material, and her stupid curly wig just in case she needed it.

Grandpa drove her back to the city and gave her a big bear hug before he drove away with tears in his eyes.

From then on, she bummed rides, hitchhiked, and rode the rails to show after show. She became a familiar fixture at the concerts as one of the dancing twirler girls. One night while twirling she had visions. Visions of jewelry, pieces that she could create to earn money. To her great surprise, they became very popular.

Thelma Lou's favorite piece depicted the creation of heaven and earth. It portrayed a blue woman of heaven hovering above a green man of earth. She protected him from above and he protected her from below. That was Thelma Lou's most popular piece and so she had it tattooed on her belly where it was always with her. When Doreen was born, she created that piece of jewelry for the last time. The necklace would always remind her daughter of who she is.

Thelma Lou's reverie was broken by the sound of the pick-up truck pulling into the gravel driveway. She looked out of the window and saw the beautiful twins. She knew in her heart that it was time to make jewelry again for her new grandchildren.

Chapter 12

Worldwide News

News traveled fast about the birth of the turquoise twins. If Arty and Doreen thought they were going to get to sleep all day after arriving home, they were in for a rude shock. Even though Doreen had just given birth the day before there was no recovery rest in bed days for her.

The world was already on its way to their farm. A quick nap was all Arty got. An overwhelmed Grandpa and a stressed-out Thelma Lou had him up and fortifying the yard around their house against the mob of people arriving uninvited. Bambi, who had slept in the guest bedroom, was up and helping too, but trying not to be seen or recognized by any of the reporters or television crews.

The press had arrived right after dawn with camera crews and equipment vans. Thelma Lou and Grandpa had to force all of them to park beyond the barbed wire fence in the cows' field behind the gate. It separated the main farmhouse and tractor barn from the cow barn. The driveway out to the main road was a real problem because it led directly to the house.

Arty helped Grandpa quickly throw together a makeshift gate. It kept the cars and people away from the house and turned them into the cow field with the press. It wasn't easy especially when the annoying reporters were constantly asking Arty a lot of questions.

Next, the problem became what to do about the cows. They had a herd of about two hundred and fifty beef cows that were the main economy for the farm. The cows could escape now with the mob taking over their pasture. They had direct access to go down the road to the highway and head into town or even worse get into the neighbor's fields.

So, it was quickly decided that Grandpa and Ol' Blue in the old pickup truck and Arty on Mister Jasper would have to round up all the cows and force them into the lower field. The same field Arty and Mister Jasper had ridden over the day before.

Ol' Blue jumped out of the truck and started barking. He ran around and rushed the cows forward by biting at their heels. The press enjoyed filming the dog and the cows for early morning news shows around the world.

Then Arty realized they had to do something with the chickens. Chickens were used to wandering around the yard all day looking for worms in the flower beds. They liked sitting on the porch in the sunshine. Basically, they did whatever they wanted to do all day before going back to the hen house to roost at night.

Well, Arty and Grandpa threw up their hands and decided that chickens don't like to be told what to do. They usually don't do it even when told. So, it was decided to let the chickens do what they always do. If some hen decided to lay an egg in a reporter's baseball cap, well so be it.

The family had no idea what they were about to experience. If they thought chickens were hard to manage, they did not understand what a mob of people could do to a farm. People were already on their way. Tons and tons of people.

The family decided Arty would guard the front porch. Grandpa and Bambi would guard the back porch. Thelma Lou would keep the babies safe from the crowds inside the house, and hopefully, give the new mother at least a few more hours of rest. That was the plan. This family thrived on peace and quiet. That was all over for them today.

The road out of town was packed with cars from all over the state of Louisiana and other surrounding states. The

I-10 highway from New Orleans to Baton Rouge was bumper-to-bumper traffic all headed to tiny Rainbow City then out the two-lane road to the farm.

The Turner family from Alabama had been traveling since dawn in a white pickup truck. They were almost to the Welcome to Rainbow City sign near where the babies were born. In the back of their truck, half a dozen kids in shorts and jeans bounced around excitedly to be on a trip out of their small town. They were windblown from flying down the highway. Their faces were covered in dust. The excitement they felt was on full display as they rumbled around the floor of the truck like crazy kids do, with no fear of falling out.

Their mama, in a plain sack dress and a teased-up hairdo, kept hanging out the window yelling "Timmy sit down and the rest of you all hold on tight and behave yourselves."

"Yes, mama." They all replied. Which of course, they had absolutely no intention of doing. The father, driving in traffic was now moving slowly as a tortoise crawls, was a mess of aggravated nerves. Yet he felt thrilled beyond control. He sat wearing his best working boots and a clean pair of overalls that were already sticky wet with sweat from the Louisiana humidity and heat. He was usually plowing a field rather than going to see aliens. But then again, how many times in life would a person really get a chance to see a live alien baby?

In front of them in a fancy yellow convertible, a city slicker kind of guy and his gal sat stalled in traffic. The driver, Henry Scroggins, all duded up in fancy cowboy boots and expensive attire fidgeted in his seat. Exasperated, he constantly blew his horn, bellowing at the cars in front of him, and acting like a total jerk.

Sitting beside him was a debutante from New Orleans, Miss Misty-Belle Lee in her best white summer outfit. She noticed the old farmer who owned the barn busy putting up a cardboard sign with *Alien Babies Born Here* printed with a magic marker. "Henry, sugar, I wonder if that man is going to charge admission to see inside that barn?"

"He ain't gonna make much if he does." The dude snorted. "Not when ya can see the real live babies right down the road." They moved an inch or two in that direction as he spoke.

The field across from the family farmhouse was now packed with cars and trucks everywhere. That was what caused the traffic to back up on the highway. There was no room for more cars. People had to pull off the side of the road and walk to the farm.

Folks who had gotten there early were unpacking folding chairs and picnic lunches they had brought.

They were spreading out all over the fields. The bigger kids ran around tossing footballs, throwing frisbees, and playing baseball.

The younger kids were blowing bubbles, rolling beach balls, and forcing their mama to find someplace they could go potty. Which was not easy as this was not Jazz Fest with its hundreds of port-a-potties lined up for folks to use. Grandpa's cornfields were getting well fertilized.

It was a different mob than the night before. This was a joyous affair celebrating the birth of the turquoise babies. The biggest event to happen in Louisiana in a long time and in Rainbow City ever. The mayor had gone on the news and invited the world to come to Rainbow City and the world had come.

Many town folks stayed up all night plotting ways to make money off of it any way they could. Dina's Diner downtown was packing to-go lunches and selling them like hotcakes. Guys with ice coolers had filled them with water, cokes, and other assorted beverages and headed out to the farm. Their business was thriving.

A neighboring farmer drove his old tractor-trailer into the middle of the field. Sitting on his make-shift stage were a few bales of hay and a local Cajun band playing "You are My Sunshine."

The crowd started singing along and cheered when the song was over. Then, the band started, "When the Saints Come Marching in" and the crowd went wild.

Of course, it would not be Louisiana without a group of loud protesters with signs. One sign was painted with ET's Go Home. Didn't they realize these babies were home? Another man's sign read God Didn't Make Turquoise Babies, but who in the world did he think made them?

A different group, on the other hand, had signs that read We Love You Babies and Turquoise is my Favorite Color. One young couple was so clever that they quickly made t-shirts with turquoise alien babies' faces on them. They sold out in no time.

Television news crews and mobs of people were now camped outside the barbed wire fence surrounding the farmhouse. No one seemed to actually know what to expect. For whatever reason, they were just there. Maybe to take a selfie and post it online and pray that it went viral. Maybe to witness a miracle. Maybe simply to say they were there and did it. For some, maybe it was to just get out of the dadburn house for a day and do something different.

Chapter 13

The Event

Grandpa was fidgeting sitting on the back porch with his bow and arrows, guarding the house. Bambi sat near him, veiled by a scarf. They talked in sign language and both belly-laughed at whatever joke Grandpa had just told her. Neither one was actually sure what they were supposed to do if the mob decided to storm the house, but they sat there anyway.

Arty knew what he was going to do. The long front porch of the yellow-painted farmhouse was filled with rocking chairs. He sat rocking with his slingshot in his hand and a big bag of marbles in the other, guarding the front of the house. He had hung tin cans along the barbed wire fence, in addition to many cowbells. Anytime anyone tried to climb through the barbed wire, a cowbell clanged, and the sound grabbed Arty's attention. Arty would stand up with his slingshot in his hand and look menacing and mean and walk the porch like a guard. Nobody was going to mess with him.

That young smarty pants in the yellow convertible, Henry, and his gal Misty-Belle decided they were going to crawl through the fence and make a video with his cell phone. When they did this, it set off the cowbells. Arty shot a marble from his slingshot and hit the can next to them.

Misty-Belle changed her mind and decided to go back. But Henry quickly handed her his phone. He tried to climb back through the barbed wire but caught and ripped his expensive shirt off. Even worse, his fancy pants were really tangled in the barbed wire.

Arty shot another marble and another can fell next to Henry. This scared him so bad that he pushed his way through the wire leaving his ripped pants dangling on the fence. He stood up and realized he was naked except for his cowboy boots and his tighty-whities underwear. Several people around him burst out laughing. They laughed even louder when he ran off in shame.

Misty-Belle got the whole episode on the phone video and posted it online. It went viral. The press camera crews had filmed it too and folks all over the world were laughing at poor Henry. Arty wagged his finger in their direction and went back to rocking. Nobody else tried to get through the barbed wire fence.

The crowd was actually more restrained by the barbed wire fence than Arty had at first thought they would be. He kept imagining a mob with torches and pitchforks like in the old Frankenstein movies. This mob seemed to feel they were here more for a party than to kill the twins. Arty liked that idea.

All these people he realized were here to celebrate the birth of his babies. It made him feel proud. It made him feel special for the first time in his life. He wondered what his brother would think of him now. If only he could see me now, Arty thought to himself. Little did he realize his brother was a few feet away looking right at him.

Several television equipment trucks were parked slightly away from the crowds. Each had its station logo and call letters on the side. All were the same, except for station WWPU. Their van looked extremely out of date from another era. The lettering was recently spray-painted over the old station's logo in a quick and unprofessional manner. There was also a big peace sign painted on the back. No one in the crowd really cared.

Sulking inside the van was Victor, who did care. After crashing the taco truck into the Mississippi River, he had to concoct a new plan. He and Winebombs were now disguised as a television news crew. They sat watching a new wall of monitors, but mainly Victor watched Arty.

"What an idiot," Victor gagged out loud, as he watched his twin brother strut around on his porch like a peacock. "The pig farmer is wearing torn jean shorts, flip-flops, a Saints t-shirt, and cap, and he is holding a stupid slingshot—not a rifle or a shotgun—a slingshot. He's shooting marbles at tin cans on a fence with cowbells. It makes me want to puke. My brother is an embarrassment to the family."

"Right now, he's world-famous," Winebombs quipped. Victor could never have admitted it, but he was jealous.

Then, Victor looked around and thought to himself about where he was and what he was doing at this moment. "I'm hiding out in a cow field, in a forty-year-old television truck with a peace sign painted on the back window. How humiliating—a peace sign. We're forced to use out-of-date military equipment and I'm sitting here waiting for something, anything to happen. I should be in my lab torturing people," he sighed.

He had made himself completely miserable. He turned to Winebombs and asked "Where did the military come up with this old piece of junk? We stand out like a sore thumb."

"It was used in a recent movie shoot here in Louisiana."

"What era was the movie set in? The civil war?" Victor snarled, trying to be funny.

"I think the seventies," Winebombs replied.

"That explains the peace sign on the back! People are pointing at that sign painted in those bright day-glow colors and laughing at us. Does that sound like we are unsuspicious and blending in with the crowd?"

"It was the best we could do under such duress and on such short notice."

"I feel like an idiot. We should be wearing clown noses."

"I'm sure no one has even noticed."

About that time, a couple banged on the door and laughed. "Hey dude, love the peace sign."

"Must be a PBS station." The woman chuckled as the two of them walked away.

"See, people notice," Victor became rabid with anger as he looked over at Winebombs. "Nobody has noticed, huh? Everybody has noticed. Clown noses, I tell you we need clown noses."

"Calm down, sir. Operation Wise Men is in progress." She pointed to one of the screens. "Let's hope your big idea works."

"Of course, it will work. I'm a genius. Why shouldn't it work? Opium for the masses. fake news. The only way it won't work is if they serve some blasted lemon jelly donuts!" He snapped.

"At least we can get better camera coverage in the house, once Bobo gets inside."

"You mean Bozo" he smirked.

She pointed. "There they are now."

The view on the screen revealed a military team of jeeps, leading an ostentatious, long black limo with American flags flapping in the wind.

Two motorcycle cops led with their blue lights flashing and their sirens blowing at full volume. They forced most of the cars and trucks off the road into the ditch to allow the caravan to pass.

They came to the billboard reading: Welcome to Rainbow City.

Behind the limo, a local police car sat flashing its blue lights. Inside, Barney, the local cop, chatted with the wolf woman from Victor's lab whose real name was Bitzy Bloom. She wore military attire instead of a police uniform. Barney seemed confused. "I don't understand exactly what you are doing here with me."

Bitzy was acting her heart out on her first assignment for Victor. She showed her badge. "Secret Service," she asserted, "I'm with the F.B.I., Buster, just in case these folk's kids are real aliens. I'm armed and ready to battle them with my mini-missile thruster." She showed him a weird sci-fi prop obviously from a locally-shot, low-budget, space adventure.

Barney started to feel really important. "Wow, I never worked with a real FBI agent before." Suddenly the procession came to an abrupt stop. The limo had slammed on the brakes and Barney almost crashed into the back of it.

"Watch it, you'll mess up my makeup" Bitzy snapped.

The two motorcycle cops in front had stopped their bikes and dismounted.

The pickup truck with the Turner family from Alabama had overheated. Smoke billowed from its radiator. The limo stopped behind them. The two motorcycle cops helped the father push the truck off the road into the ditch as little Timmy the youngest son watched in disappointment. The motorcycle cops started blaring their sirens and the entourage started on its way again.

Several younger kids in the back started cheering and waving American flags to the military and passengers in the limo as it passed them now. The poor father looked exasperated at his smoking truck, now stuck in a ditch after their long drive. He realized they were going to miss all the fun.

Chapter 14

Victor's Plan

The limousine arrived with great fanfare at the family farmhouse.

The local high school band had gotten off their school bus hours ago. They had been standing at alert in their hot wool uniforms in the blazing sun. On this humid, miserable Louisiana day they finally got their big moment. They went into action, marching in front of the limo as it reached its destination.

The drum major, Eugene Guidry, a tall lanky teenager, fastened the buckle on his tall wool hat, blew his whistle, and raised his baton over his head. Sixteen beautifully coiffed majorettes started twirling their batons as the band burst into the Christmas song "We Three Kings." Just like everything they played it sounded like a rousing march written by John Philip Sousa.

Arty stood up and walked to the top steps of the front porch in amazement. He loved a parade. Grandpa and

Bambi ran around from the backyard to see what the heck was going on. Seeing the important look of this grand parade, unknowingly Grandpa ran and opened the gate so the spectacle could enter the yard.

The excited crowd in the field went wild applauding and cheering. It was everything they had hoped for and more. Now they knew they were going to see the turquoise twins. They were all so glad they had come. Finally, something was happening.

The band continued to play and Grandpa's rooster, General Patton, came marching around the side of the house with several hens running around him wanting to be part of the excitement.

In the WWPU van, a very satisfied Victor smiled as his plan unfolded before him.

Winebombs, impressed, looked at him, "You know your brother well."

"He's never missed a Mardi Gras parade in his life."

They did a high five to celebrate their success.

Now in the driveway of the front yard, the band finished. A rotund, pig of a man, Mayor Weidican, made a grand entrance as he stepped out of the limo. He walked the length of the fence playing for the crowd and media cameras delivering a full-on political performance. He was a Louisiana-born ham, and this would be the greatest moment of his political career.

"Ladies and Gentlemen," he called out to the crowd in a booming voice, "On this joyous occasion, it is my great honor to introduce Two Wise Men and One Wise Woman, who have traveled from across the globe to bring gifts of great value to our magnificent turquoise twins of Rainbow City."

Then a drum roll from the band as applause, screams, and cheers rang out from the crowd.

The mayor continued, "— his high holy mystic, Baba Baksheesh Baba Dosha."

Baba Dosha got out of the limo and bowed. It was really Trumbo from Victor's lab in makeup and a red Buddhist high lama costume.

"His gift is..." the mayor paused for dramatic effect, "a twelve-volume transformational meditation DVD set in 3-D and Blu-Ray, guaranteed to bring nirvana to anyone who watches."

The crowd oohed and ahhed. One woman remarked to another, "It's better than *The Secret.*"

"And from Zixterrialand..." the mayor went on again.

Inside the farmhouse den, Doreen stumbled out of her bedroom in her slippers and one of Arty's cut-off T-shirts. She was running her fingers through her hair and yawned trying to wake up. "What the heck is all the noise? I can't get any sleep."

Thelma Lou sat with Willow and Scooter glued to the television watching the movie *Village of the Damned*. On the screen, white-haired children were controlling a man using their evil eyes. Scooter squinted his face imitating the children on screen. Willow watched him amazed, then tried it herself.

"Wow, what if the twins have special powers like that?" Doreen asked, pulling on her jeans and boots.

"Shut your mouth," Thelma Lou warned. "That's all we need. Remember, powers have to be controlled."

The back door opened, and Bambi entered. "Are you getting a load of this farce happening out front?"

Thelma Lou shook her head, "No, we're watching a nice movie about children."

Bambi walked over and changed the channel with the remote. "Well, three so-called wise persons have arrived with gifts."

Doreen got concerned. "There are camels in our front yard?"

"What next?" Thelma Lou muttered as she held the twins a little closer.

They watched the television as the mayor applauded and the fake Zixterrialand representative bowed. It was really Fat Sam in a grand who-knows-what outfit.

"And, last but not least," the mayor barked out, "our own gambling goddess, Yacanna-Notta-Toucha-Me from the Whatta-Scama-Rooni Casino and Playland Resort.

This gift is a three-day, all-expense-paid vacation and one hundred Scama-Rooni gambling chips. Plus—plus—ringside seats at the goddess' live show, *We Are All Children of the Rainbow*.

The crowd went wild as the goddess, in full Vegas-style showgirl costume, exited the limo. She was actually Dana LaFossie in disguise. She demonstrated why she was a success as a game show hostess. She pointed, she posed, and she pranced with great skill.

The high school band played "Away in a Manger," but it too sounded like a Sousa march. The phony wise people hammed it up to the cheering crowd.

Inside, the family was watching the scene outside on their television screen. First on the screen, then out the window. Back and forth like a ping pong game. It was starting to dawn on them that what they were seeing on the screen was not a movie but reality happening in their own front yard.

"Bambi, this is better than 3-D," Thelma Lou joked before she turned to her daughter. "Doreen, "Get to your station soldier." Doreen walked to a gigantic gun case containing an arsenal of weapons.

"Go help Arty, there are gifts being delivered to the front porch," Bambi told Doreen.

Doreen grabbed a gun, loaded it, and headed to the porch. "Haven't they heard of Federal Express?"

Outside, Arty was watching the mayor and the three wise person's parade across the lawn.

Doreen stepped out of the house and next to Arty. She aimed her gun.

The mayor and the three wise persons reached the house steps.

"When did the circus come to town?" She asked the mayor.

He continued the show, not taking her seriously. "These great and important persons are here to see the turquoise babies." He explained.

"They'll see hell sooner." She threatened, then gave Arty a glance.

Arty reluctantly pointed his slingshot at them too.

The mayor took his foot off the first step and backed up slowly. "They bring extraordinary gifts."

"Like the Trojan Horse. We don't need no gifts from no gurus." Doreen answered, then turned to Arty, "Ain't that right Arty?"

"I don't know," Arty stammered, "I was kind of excited about those meditation DVDs, I've always liked that band, Nirvana."

The mayor tried to take another step up onto the porch Arty got upset and stopped him.

"Oh, no. Wait." Arty cried out.

Everyone and everything stopped in a panic.

Arty got down on his knees and scooped up a spider, moved it out of the way, just in time, so it didn't get squashed. "Okay, it's okay now," relieved, Arty stepped back onto the porch next to Doreen.

In the WWPU van, Victor griped. "Did he just save a stupid spider on live television? I hate that little goody-two-shoes."

Doreen pointed her gun at the mayor again. Arty quickly got ready for action with his marble and slingshot.

"Not one step closer," Doreen warned.

"Doreen, the whole world is watching you on live television, sweetheart. All they want is to see the twins." The mayor explained with desperation in his voice, he was pleading with her. All eyes were on the porch. The suspense was chilling.

Inside the WWPU van, Victor stood banging on the monitors. Their view was far away but was getting closer and closer as Winebombs controlled two bug drones flying over the crowd.

"Get those drone cameras closer," Victor demanded. Winebombs sent the two drones flying towards the house. It was a standoff at the porch.

Bambi and Thelma Lou came out of the house each carrying one of the twins. Suddenly, the crowd gasped in shock. Their faces filled with awe. A hush fell across the entire field in unison.

TIME stood still.

Everyone was mesmerized by the light emanating from Willow and Scooter, who joyfully embraced the audience with their eyes.

The mayor's mouth dropped open in amazement. Dana froze in place, Trumbo dropped his hat, Fat Sam exclaimed "Geeze they're really real."

In the field, one of the protesters dropped her sign and bowed in reverence. Misty-Belle burst into tears and grabbed Henry's hand. He pulled her close and gave her a hug.

Even Victor and Winebombs in the van sat motionless realizing this was a moment that was changing all who were there to witness it. They had completely forgotten about the drones.

The crowd started cheering, applauding, and screaming with joy. The news cameras never stopped running and shared the moment across the world. Everyone on planet earth saw the live, giggling, happy turquoise babies waving their little turquoise hands.

The band played "God Bless America."

Suddenly the two drones flew towards Doreen's face. She swatted at them thinking they were bugs, "Those dadblamed bugs again."

"Those are not real bugs," Arty hollered. "Get the babies inside."

Arty pointed his slingshot at the drones and fired a marble—the drone exploded.

Everyone screamed. Bambi and Thelma Lou quickly ran inside safely with the babies.

Arty reloaded another marble. He shot the other drone—it exploded.

The crowd panicked and erupted into chaos; they were breaking down the fence. The cowbells rattling, the tin cans falling, people started scattering in all directions. They got in their cars and drove away.

The police and media cameramen headed towards the action at the front porch.

The monitors went blank in the WWPU van.

Winebombs shouted to Victor. "Holy snot, two million dollars' worth of equipment blasted by a slingshot."

Victor snickered, "With a marble—that's my brother."

Chapter 15

The Fly

In town at Beauregard and his daughter Sally Ann's house, Beauregard stood in his underwear folding laundry and watching the news.

On his television, Barney and Bitzy were arresting Arty who was handcuffed, frisked, and pushed into a police car. Doreen beat on the police car. Barney grabbed her; Bitzy pointed her laser gun at Doreen.

Beauregard stopped what he was doing and yelled at the screen. "Who is that woman cop? That should've been me. Everybody tells me I should be a movie star. Just look at this face." He gazed lovingly at his own reflection on the screen. "I wanna be on TV; that should've been me." He was on his knees in front of the television almost in tears.

On the screen, Doreen gave Barney a karate chop and a kick. He doubled over in pain, and she escaped.

"He's getting beat up by the mother," Beauregard raged at the television. "And that stupid woman is shooting"— He looked closer at the screen— "A ray gun?"

At the farm, Doreen got in Arty's pickup truck. It did not start. The police car pulled out of the gate with Arty inside. Doreen leapt out and ran to the barn, jumping bareback onto Mister Jasper, "Gitty-up Mister Jasper, we got to save Arty."

Mr. Jasper raced down the driveway, out onto the road, and followed the police car.

As Beauregard watched, a newscaster told the story as it unfolded. "As you can see, the man responsible, Arty Wood, is being taken away now. His wife, the mother of the notorious turquoise twins, just took off on a horse without a saddle. Wow, look at her go. We recently learned the mother did two combat tours of duty in Afghanistan."

Mister Jasper was gaining on the police car. Bitzy was hanging out of the window pretending she was shooting laser beams from her mini-missile thruster towards the horse. "Take that—and that!" She howled each time she pulled the trigger and, of course, nothing at all happened.

Back at the Dingledorper's house, Sally Ann entered in elaborate face make-up and a full-on Madonna outfit. She had fashioned a bra out of two snow cone cups that she had painted with gold leaf. She jumped in front of the television and started to dance and sing "Express Yourself" which blocked her dad's view.

Her father shoved her out of the way. He was frantic. Outraged. "Get out of the way, Sally Ann, and shut up, I should've been there. I could have been beat up live on worldwide news."

Sally Ann stomped her feet. She was so mad that she threw a vase of flowers across the room.

"You oughta be hogtied young lady," he replied flatly without looking up from the television.

"Forget those turquoise babies, Daddy! I'm the star of this town." She ran out the back door and slammed it behind her.

She stormed across the backyard on a mission, talking to herself as she went. "Today it's not good enough to be young, beautiful, and talented, you gotta be a weird color too!"

Her father came to the back door, "Get back in here, Sally Ann, and take your medication."

Sally Ann did not slow down or listen to him. "Go iron my costumes, Daddy. I am done with that medication. It just calms me down. I need all my talents today. Now, I have a performance to give."

Sally Ann walked past the town police station and into a grocery store. Her tap shoes could be heard tapping clickity-clank. Sally Ann walked into the place like she owned it.

Several lady customers saw her and rolled their eyes. She was obviously well known and disliked in town. A busy body gossiped to the cashier. "That little girl is a bad seed." The cashier shook her head in agreement.

Sally Ann went past the laundry detergent and right to the clothing dye section. She stopped and spotted a bottle of purple dye. She tried to reach it but couldn't. She desperately looked around for help, whimpering like a baby.

Old Clem, the 80-year-old owner of the grocery store, stopped his sweeping and went to her. "You needin' some help, little lady?"

Sally Ann batted her eyes and over-acted like an Actor's Studio graduate in a Tennessee Williams movie. "Ol' Clem, sugar, could you be a darlin' and fetch me that bottle of purple dye right there?"

He got it for her.

"Could you grab a few more bottles, sugar?"

"As long as you ain't buyin' rat poison again. Don't want them to put you back into that mental institution."

"I'm about to become a world-famous star! I'm getting too big for this little town." She waved goodbye and blew a kiss. Laughing deviously and tap dancing furiously, Sally Ann rushed out of the grocery store to avoid paying for the purple dye.

"I guess I'm supposed to put it on her daddy's tab." the cashier commented as she made a note of it.

In spite of the blaring sirens, she danced and spun across Main Street oblivious to the police car that was carrying Arty to the police station. Barney saw Sally Ann just in time and slammed on his brakes as the car spun out of control taking a fire hydrant with it.

Barney jumped out of the car, threw his hat to the ground, and jumped on it in frustration. "Dagburnit Sally Ann ya think you're the only person on the planet. Ya almost got us all kilt. Who do ya think you are!"

Not missing a beat Sally Ann continued to tap dance down the street. She flung herself into a crazy pirouette and cackled like a hen. "Why Barney, just you wait and see, you, this town, and the whole world will know who I am before you know it."

Sally Ann ran home, through the yard, up the stairs, past her daddy who was now ironing one of her dresses, and into the bathroom. She went straight to the bathtub and turned on the hot water. Within a few minutes, steam was rising from the tub. She poured in the purple dye and swished it around with her hand. When she took her hand out, it was dyed bright purple. She squealed in delight.

Before she could ready herself to jump in the tub there was a terrible ruckus and she hurried to the bathroom window to see what was going on.

From her window, she could see a furious Barney. Various car parts continued to fall from his car. A bewildered, shaken Arty was removed from the back seat.

Bitzy Bloom, the wolf woman, pressed her mini-missile thruster into his ribs. "Don't make a move, buster or my ray gun will vaporize you quick." She tossed her hair for good effect and growled a wolf growl.

Barney grabbed Arty's other arm, and they roughly escorted him into the police station.

Arty did as he was told.

Once again, Sally Ann turned towards the bathtub when she was distracted by Doreen who was riding Mister Jasper outside on the street. They galloped their way to the station followed by several police cars blaring their sirens. Media vans, trucks, and car loads of curious people were behind them.

Sally Ann slammed the window shut and turned back to the tub to continue with her dastardly plan.

Mister Jasper slid into the police station driveway like a pro baseball player sliding into home base. Doreen jumped off of the horse and headed into the police station.

Inside Arty was being booked. He felt helpless. The media was filming it all, he paid no attention to them.

Linda Comeaux, the small-time local news anchor and her camera crew pressed in on Arty's personal space. They were trying to get a good shot of him as he was being ushered out of the area by Barney and Bitzy. Failing to get a statement from Arty, Linda looked into the camera and awkwardly and took on the air of a big-time reporter.

"After he caused violent explosions of government drones and a barrage of bullets was fired into the massive crowd of innocent bystanders, Arty Wood, father of the notorious turquoise alien twins, is being put behind bars for the safety of the entire human race. They're taking him before Judge Wifflestein now."

Barney and Bitzy escorted Arty into the small-town courtroom. Bitzy noticed a No Smoking sign. That old mean Judge William Wifflestein sat impatiently in the creaky judge's chair smoking a cigarette. He took one long deep drag and reluctantly put the fire out in an ashtray.

The skeletal old man looked down his long thin nose where his glasses rested perilously at the tip, threatening to drop to the floor at any moment. He was swatting a buzzing fly.

The judge peered at Arty with the same perpetual look of disgust that had settled on his face years ago. He pointed a bony finger at Arty and waved it around as if to put a hex on him.

"This is the man who attacked me, Your Honor." Barney moaned to the judge as he pointed to poor Arty standing beside him.

"What, you attacked a police officer? Well, did ya, son?" The judge asked Arty.

"Well, I guess I did," Arty started, "but—"

The judge cut him off. "—No, buts in here. Either you did or you didn't."

The fly that was annoying the judge buzzed around his face and landed on his glasses. He waved it away. It flew around his head faster and noisier. The judge was becoming more concerned with the fly than with Arty.

Barney interrupted the judge's battle with the fly to continue his protest against Arty. "After he shot down two expensive bug things."

"Bug things?" The judge inquired, becoming increasingly more annoyed.

"Well sir, they look like bugs, but they are cameras."

"Yes," Bitzy added. "He shot down two expensive bug things the government agents were using for surveillance. I know because I am an undercover for the FBI," she showed her fake badge.

The judge sighed at Barney and Bitzy's abject ignorance and impatiently shot back. "Drones? You mean military drones?" He swatted the fly again and again. It was driving him crazy. "Where did I drop that swatter?" He muttered to himself as he searched behind his desk for it. "Why was the military using drones to spy on this man?" The judge asked as he rose again. This time with an old fly swatter made out of screen wire in his hand.

Barney leaned forward knowingly. "Well, ya know your honor, he's the alien that fathered them there turquoise babies that's causing all the trouble in our once peaceful town. I didn't get no sleep last night with all the people calling me and complaining about aliens."

The judge was outraged, he looked at Arty as he kept swatting the fly. "So, it's you causing all this! What have you got to say for yourself?"

The judge kept banging the fly swatter on the desk. Right in front of Arty's eyes he swatted the fly and tried to kill it, but it was still not dead. It was stuck on the fly swatter writhing in pain. "Help me! Help me!" cried the fly sensing Arty's compassion.

Arty gasped. He was so upset about the creature's plight that he forgot about his own predicament. His eyes filled with tears, but he could do nothing to save it; he was in handcuffs. "Poor little fly." Arty sobbed, distressed by the senseless attack on the insect's life.

The judge took his gavel and slammed it down on the fly, killing it dead, right in front of Arty, who wept uncontrollably. "You killed an innocent creature."

The judge was horrified that a grown man could weep for a fly. "He must be insane." roared the judge. "Lock him up."

Arty couldn't believe his ears, "but my family your honor please" Arty entreated through his tears.

"Crying won't help you, or the fly. You're not an alien, you're a dadblam liberal snowflake!" The judge was finished with the stupid fly and with Arty. "Throw him in a cell and lose the key."

Barney was gleeful at the results of his testimony. "With pleasure, yes, siree, your honor." Barney pushed Arty out into the hallway, with the wolf woman and her phony sci-fi gun in tow.

Judge William Wifflestein vigorously pounded the gavel on his desk once more. "Court adjourned!"

Chapter 16

Surprise

I n the lobby of the police station, Doreen burst through the door into the crowd blocking the reception desk. The newswoman, Linda Comeaux, stuck a microphone into Doreen's face. Linda smugly turned to the live broadcast camera.

"That's the mother who gave birth to the demons."

"Move it, bimbo!" Doreen pushed through the crowd and yelled above the clamor. "Arty, I'll save you." She rushed forward and some of the police restrained her.

Doreen pleaded with the police as a cameraman broke through the crowd and got right in her face. Doreen avoided the camera as she tried to explain the events of the arrest to the police that were keeping her in check.

"He wasn't shooting at anybody. Arty wouldn't hurt a fly. Those were fake bugs he shot with a slingshot. I was the one with the gun. Arrest me." The cameraman maneuvered his way into Doreen's space once again.

Doreen reacted intensely. "Get out my face, sewer breath!"

Not deterred by Doreen's wrath, the cameraman pressed her for more answers. "What planet are you from?"

Doreen turned on him frustrated and disgusted. "Louisiana—born and bred."

The police forced the cameraman away from Doreen, but not for long. He focused the lens on the reporter of the day, Linda, who continued her broadcast. "Hysterical and apparently as deranged as her husband, the mother still claims she was not abducted by aliens. We have Professor Smith of Columbia University here to explain…"

Before Professor Smith could appear on the broadcast, suddenly, Linda stopped speaking, there was a scream. All of the media attention shifted as Sally Ann entered the police station, purple as a ripe grape. Her skin was dyed bright purple and she wore a gold bikini bottom with her gold snow cone Madonna top.

Thrilled to be back in the spotlight Sally Ann had upped the ante with a brand-new act. It was a bizarre mixture of Lady Gaga, Pink, and the vaudeville comedienne Fanny Brice all rolled into one. With all eyes on her, she began to gather the crowd with all of the grace of a sideshow barker.

"Gather round y'all, because you see, I'm an alien too. Yahoo! Yahoo! Why do you think we call it Rainbow City? We are all aliens here!" Now that she had everybody's attention, she began a song and dance number that led with a golden oldie "Color My World with Sunshine" and led right into a chorus of "Let the Sunshine In" from the musical *Hair*. She was in her glory as everybody in the space joined in her performance. The cameras were rolling, and the spotlight was now on Sally Ann, and she was determined to keep it that way.

Linda Comeaux swayed with the music as she wrapped up her reporting for the broadcast. "You heard it live folks, apparently there's an alien invasion! The whole town has been taken over by aliens."

Back at Grandpa's farmhouse, the television was on with the sound turned down. Grandpa and Thelma Lou wanted to keep track of the news and what was going on with Doreen and Arty.

The twins were in their baby bed near the kitchen table where Grandpa sat trying to teach them to move a pencil with their minds. They seemed to understand him. Thelma Lou shook her head. She was irritated with Grandpa when she saw what he was doing. He read her lips as she scolded him.

"Will you stop that? They are newborn babies. Have you gone nuts?"

Grandpa interrupted the lessons and signed in response to Thelma Lou. "They might have special powers." Grandpa signed.

She attempted to push him out of the room. "Special powers! Get out of here. They are as normal as I am."

Grandpa ducked away from her on the way out of the room, but he couldn't help but take one more walk past the babies' bed to share a laugh with them. Grandpa and the babies made faces at Thelma Lou's *normal* description of all of them. Thelma Lou pointed again at the exit and with the bossiness of mothers and grandmothers the world over, she ended the discussion with one word, — "Out."

This time Grandpa complied but not without a chuckle under his breath as he left the room.

Thelma Lou watched him go, then turned back to the twins just in time to see two pencils move across the table, stand on end and spin as Willow and Scooter tried to outdo each other. Thelma Lou turned her attention to the giggling babies.

"Oh no, do not do that. Put those pencils back." She pointed and the pencils moved back into place. She leaned into the babies' faces and looked them both in their eyes with a warning. "Listen to me. Do not listen to

Grandpa, he's only human. You cannot let people know what you are."

Just then the phone rang. Thelma Lou picked it up and sat down at the kitchen table. It was Doreen calling from the police station where she was being guarded from the heckling media by two police officers. She spoke as loud as she could over the chaos. "Mama it's a war zone down here."

Thelma Lou's voice immediately filled with concern as she heard the stress in her daughter's voice, "Are you ok, baby girl? What's going on with you? Do you need Grandpa or me to come down there?"

Doreen's eyes filled with tears, she really did want her mom, but she knew if she broke down now, she was lost. "I'm ok Mama, I can handle this place on my own. What I need most from you is to make sure my babies are safe and that everything is calm there."

Thelma Lou knew Doreen wasn't ready to take on the new information about the unexpected progress of her newborn twins.

"Is everything okay there, Mama?"

Thelma Lou decided to change the subject. "What about Arty, baby girl? Did they lock him up?"

Doreen tried to answer but just then the crowd roared in approval at the somersaults and cartwheels that Sally Ann was doing across the desks at the station. On top of that, the cameraman continued to harass Doreen as she attempted to turn away. "What Mama? I can't hear you."

"Arty? What's going on with Arty?"

"I haven't seen him Mama, but they're bringing him out soon. I'm trying to get the charges dropped. Some horrible purple child thinks she's an alien. it's insane here."

Thelma Lou turned to check on the twins just in time to see the box of pencils open. Pencils flew out and started circling around the room. Thelma Lou panicked and scolded the twins.

"Stop that right now, both of you!"

When Doreen heard her mother yell she got concerned. She turned away from the cameras, but the one cameraman raced around for another close-up.

"Mama? What's the matter?"

Thelma Lou silently berated herself for slipping up and adding this to Doreen's problems. She looked up and saw Sally Ann on the television screen in the kitchen and made a quick recovery. "Oh, nothing darling, nothing. That little tap-dancing freak is Beauregard's little girl, Sally Ann. She just got out of the nuthouse for feeding the little Parker boy rat poison. He didn't die, but he was sure sick for a few days. He was becoming a little league football star and stealing her spotlight. She's a little monster, but she's got talent."

Thelma Lou grabbed the pencils and put them in a drawer. Then the napkins in a holder on the kitchen table started to lift up, one by one, and float towards her. The twins laughed out loud. Thelma Lou started grabbing napkins.

At the police station, Doreen snorted, "Talent! You call that talent. I call that annoying."

"That's nice dear?" Thelma Lou had lost her train of thought.

Doreen started to answer but the cameraman was moving in again. Doreen's eyes narrowed and she started to move threateningly towards him. "Back off garlic breath." He backed away but kept the camera on her. She bristled.

Meanwhile back in the kitchen, Thelma Lou grabbed napkin after napkin as they flew at her. She desperately tried to concentrate on the call with her daughter.

"Will y'all be home soon? I'm cooking Tuna Helper and Jello salad for dinner. Y'all also want Tater Tots with that?"

Doreen wasn't buying Thelma Lou's ruse. "Something's the matter with the twins, isn't it? What's going on?"

A second cameraman broke through the crowd and was able to film Doreen as she threatened the first cameraman.

"Mama these paparazzi are everywhere" Doreen turned around angrily. "Get outta here before I slug both of you! Sorry, Mama, I wasn't talkin' to you."

Thelma Lou's attention to Doreen had disappeared. Panic crossed Thelma Lou's face as cabinet doors slammed open and shut and plates flew around the room. In the middle of the twins' shenanigans, Thelma Lou saw Doreen's image playing on the television now and she ran to it as she talked to her daughter. "I can see you on TV talking to me on the phone. How amazing." She looked closer at her daughter "You look tired darling. You need a new hairdo."

Doreen was distracted at the moment; she had both cameramen backing up and she was losing it. "Quit filming me scuzz balls." They ain't stopping mama. What do you mean by a new hairdo? Of course, my hair is a mess, I just rode into town on a horse."

Thelma Lou was battling plates, catching them one by one as she struggled with the phone, but nonetheless, her maternal instinct kicked in anyway. "Watch your language young lady. The whole church probably heard you say scuzz balls."

"What? Mama, I don't give a hoot what your church women think. I can't help it if they all get their panties in a bunch over scuzz balls."

Having caught all the plates, Thelma Lou put them on the counter. That did it! Doreen had crossed the line and the expression on Thelma Lou's face and the tone in her voice meant she had reached the end of sweet mama tolerance and everybody better scatter. "Young Lady, y'all better wash your mouth out with soap for thinking such things!"

Doreen took it all in and knew she had pushed her mom to the limit and continued resigned, "Okay Mother, I'll get a new haircut," and then added meekly, "but please not a perm."

Thelma Lou softened and chuckled, "I do love you, baby girl."

"I love you more Mama, I'm just worried about what they might be doing to my poor sweet Arty. Hold on Mama, something's happening, it's getting wild here, the press is going crazy."

This time they weren't surrounding Doreen. The police escort brought Arty out from the back. He was still in handcuffs.

A cop blocked Doreen from going to him. "They're bringing Arty out now. Poor Arty."

Thelma Lou was so excited that she ran to the television and turned up the volume. "Yes, I see him." Enthralled with the image on the screen Thelma Lou absent-mindedly brushed away an imaginary insect. Soon it became crystal clear that there was no insect. There were plates, napkins, and pencils dancing a fully staged ballet around Thelma Lou as she stood watching. Thelma Lou attempted to bring the conversation to an end. "Well, y'all have a safe drive home now, ya' hear. Tell Arty not to drive too fast. Wouldn't want him to get a ticket on live television."

"We're on a horse, Mother."

"Oh, yeah. Well, that's nice dear. Well, see ya', butterfly kisses. Bye, bye." Thelma Lou hung up abruptly.

Doreen stood looking at the phone with a puzzled expression.

Thelma Lou turned to the twins. "Children, this is unacceptable behavior. Stop immediately!" She snapped her fingers, and everything flew back into place. She had turned a vibrant blue. "Someday I'll teach you how to control this, but for now Granny is more powerful than you! Learn some discipline." Then, unexpectedly, she growled at the children, who stared back at her in wide-eyed amazement.

Grandpa walked back in reading a newspaper.

Instantly Thelma Lou's skin color and demeanor changed back to normal. She looked around. Everything was back in place. Without missing a beat Thelma Lou became the epitome of a loving grandma.

"Goldilocks was asleep when the three bears came home. Oh, look, little darlings, here's Papa Bear now, Grrr, what did you say Papa Bear when there was no porridge?"

Grandpa looked puzzled. Thelma Lou signed the question to him. Grandpa emphatically grunted out a barely audible, "Fee-fi-fo-fum".

"Fee-fi-fo-fum?" Thelma Lou mused. "Wrong Fairy Tale."

Chapter 17

Snowflake

B arney walked Arty down the corridor of the county jail. It stood right next door to the courthouse. It was very old, run-down, even rustic in an old gangster movie way. Barney opened a cell full of other convicts and pushed Arty inside.

"The judge sent you animals a liberal snowflake to devour," Barney told them as he locked Arty in the cell with a group of thugs. All the convicts reacted with rage and anger. "A snowflake!" they snorted and laughed.

They were a rough bunch of redneck motorcycle riders arrested for disturbing the peace the night before. Their leather-clad motorcycle club was named Hogs on Hogs. They were big, brawny dudes of different ages, some long-haired others were skinheads, all with bad attitudes.

The leader of the gang Butch Stubbs was dressed in all black leather with a bright pink pig symbol on his back. Being dressed in leather on a hot, humid ninety-eight-degree Louisiana day he was sweating, well, like a hog.

In a weird way, they all looked like hogs. As a group, they had lots of tattoos of hogs on their arms and nose rings in every member's nose. They were the ugliest, meanest looking group of fat men ever penned in one cell. The long, greasy-haired leader, Butch picked up Arty by the neck and got right in his face.

"You a snowflake?" He demanded to know.

"I guess," Arty replied in a high-pitched, scared voice.

All the convicts burst into laughter. Butch pushed Arty across the dark cell into a spotlight of sunshine that lit Arty as if he was on a stage.

"Ok, snowflake. Melt for us," he demanded.

Arty imitated a snowflake as it melted to the best of his ability. They all laughed.

Outside the police station, Doreen led Mister Jasper down the street and talked to the horse as if he was a person. The horse nodded and understood everything she was saying.

"I learned a few things in Afghanistan that they don't teach a woman here in high school. One, you never leave a soldier behind, even when he's captured. We're gonna get Arty outta that jail, you hear me, Mister Jasper?"

The horse nodded, he understood and whinnied. She was now in front of a hardware store.

"Arty is my man–and your man and we've got to save our man." she continued, "You stay here, I've got to buy some things we're going to need. Why they could be torturing poor Arty right now."

The horse looked sad and mad at the same time. Doreen walked into the hardware store like a marine with a plan.

At the same time, back in the jail, Arty had turned into the cell block comedian. He was doing a standup routine of different things melting, entertaining the whole gang.

"And this one is butter melting on a hot pancake." Arty performed as he did his melting bit again, this time with sound effects of the butter crackling in the pan.

The Hogs all burst out in loud laughter.

"Hey, you gotta join our bowling league," Butch said "Ain't he fellas?"

The whole gang cheered "yeah."

Arty could not wait to do another one, he was having the time of his life.

"And you know those little wax Christmas candles that look like an angel?" he asked them.

They all agreed, "Yeah."

"Well, this is that angel melting." Arty did a crazy melting angel bit.

All the convicts laughed and applauded.

Mister Jasper stood patiently waiting in front of the hardware store as Doreen exited with supplies. She carried a large thick rope, some chains and a bag full of other stuff.

"Come on. This ought to do it, Mister Jasper. I'm going to need your help. If this town wants war, then, it's time to teach this town a lesson."

She walked off with Mister Jasper and they went down a block and to the back of the jailhouse which was next door to the courthouse and behind the police station. She heard the roars of laughter coming from one of the cells and reacted. "Oh, what horrible things they must be doing to my poor sweet Arty."

She wrapped a handful of dynamite sticks together with duct tape. Then taped it to the brick wall below the bars of the window of the cell where Arty was being held inside. She knew what she was doing.

Unseen by her, inside, the Hogs were loving it, as Arty finished his imitation of an iceberg melting at sea.

The gang leader begged Arty, "Do the wicked witch from the *Wizard of Oz* again, that's my favorite. Don't you agree, boys?" They all agreed.

Arty became so excited, as folks would say in Louisiana, he was in hog heaven. "Okay, Butch but you act like you're throwing a bucket of water on me, so I can get in the mood."

The gang leader got ready and pretended to throw an imaginary bucket of water on Arty, who started melting like Margaret Hamilton the green-faced witch in the movie.

"I'm melting! Melting!" he acted out, doing a good imitation of her voice.

Doreen yelled from the alley. Everyone in the cell looked her way.

"Move away from the wall guys."

Suddenly there was a loud *Boom!*

The old brick wall of the prison cell crumbled. The gang inside saw Doreen outside the hole with the horse ready to gallop away.

Arty was in shock, but happy. "Doreen?"

"That's your gal?" Butch asked Arty.

"That's my wife," Arty beamed with pride.

"Hot dog!" Butch hollered, "I needs me one like that."

"Come on Arty, hurry up. We ain't got all day." Doreen insisted, "Let's go."

Arty climbed over the bricks into the alley. Doreen helped lift him up onto Mister Jasper and they rode off.

Butch exited the cell through the hole, then motioned for all the other Hogs to follow him out.

"Come on guys, we got us a get outta jail-free card. I done changed my mind about snowflakes!"

Squealing hogs crawled through the hole and went running in all directions. Soon all the jail cells were empty.

Chapter 18

Home Sweet Swamp

When it became obvious that Arty, Doreen, and the twins could no longer live at the farmhouse, Bambi came to the rescue. She knew she could not fly them all to her home in Malibu, California. Her French Quarter apartment would be the first place after the farm that the police and press would look.

Bambi was a clever gal, even at the beginning of her career, so she bought herself a "secret getaway" in the Atchafalaya River Basin swamp in the middle of Nowhere, Louisiana. It is one of the most beautiful spots in the world. One so isolated that even most residents of Louisiana have never ventured there.

She built a cabin in the woods which she called *The Fishing Camp.* It was a very modern, totally up-to-date home, disguised on the outside as a typical cypress wood and tin-roofed Cajun shack. It was built on sturdy piling right on the edge of the basin.

It had a porch on the waterside with a pier that jutted out twenty feet into the bayou. At the end was a boathouse with two small motorboats that hung from a pulley system allowing them to be lowered quickly into the water. When he was small, Arty and Bambi loved using a boat to go riding around the vast swamp.

They enjoyed the scenery of cathedrals of majestic, ancient cypress trees that grew fifty to one hundred feet into the air. Many of them were covered with a canopy of hanging gray moss, so thick it filtered the sunlight into glistening patterns on the still water. They loved taking a picnic lunch of peanut butter and jelly sandwiches, just spending the whole day relaxing in the calm and near silence of this peaceful place.

Victor could not have been more bored. He hated the swamp. He hated the flies, the mosquitoes, the smells of rotting algae in the stagnant water, but most of all — the boredom. He saw no beauty in nature. He had no interest in scenery or red glowing sunsets that made the water red and gold. Boring. The only frog Victor wanted to see was one that he could capture, kill and dissect.

Bambi learned very quickly that her two sons were totally opposite in almost every way. They always had separate bedrooms after they were old enough to fight each other like wild animals. "Go to your separate cages "she would tell them jokingly. But it wasn't a joke.

Victor liked being alone in his room with his chemistry set, his books, and his secret experiments. Every one of Bambi's three houses had a space they all dubbed *Victor's Lab*. No one was allowed to enter except the housekeeper who always found the room exceedingly clean, tidy and all the cabinets, drawers, and closets locked. Victor was very secretive.

All the maid had to do was clean the bathroom, change the sheets, vacuum and take out the clothes hamper to the laundry room. Victor was the most tidy, organized, and reticent child she had ever encountered.

She was extremely afraid of him. Just being in his room made her spine shiver. She did her chores as quickly as possible and got out of that room. What evil things did this wicked child do there?

He always treated her as if she were some lower-level human of the species. She despised him. Being a good Catholic, she always crossed herself and kissed the crucifix that hung around her neck before entering Victor's lab. She would breathe a deep sigh of relief as she exited and closed the door.

Arty she loved, even if his room was always a total mess with clothes and shoes scattered everywhere. He just pulled off clothes and threw them wherever they landed.

She always had to crawl under his bed looking for a stray sock or a lost shoe.

And toys, toys were everywhere, never in their box. Arty was a normal child and she enjoyed picking up after him. She loved how he never learned to put the cap on a tube of toothpaste, a thing he still never did as an adult. Arty acted like a boy who did things the way boys do.

Even when as a teenager the toys had turned into baseballs and bats, tennis rackets, and golf clubs, she enjoyed picking them up. She put them into his closet reassured that she knew everything about him. Nothing was hidden or locked up, things were always scattered all over the place for anyone to see. Such honesty she adored.

Bambi felt amused at her trusted housekeeper's opposite opinions of her two boys. They had been like a happy family or at least she thought so. Bambi had not come from a happy family.

At ten years old her father disappeared, and her mother always claimed the mob had rubbed him out because of his shady dealings. She used to say he rotted at the bottom of the Mississippi River wearing concrete boots and being nibbled on by little fishes. It was a terrible thing to tell a child. To this day Bambi still did not know the truth.

However, he had left her mother rich, living in a beautiful mansion in the Garden District of New Orleans where she enjoyed the benefits of high society. It was filled with secret societies that live in a different world of luxury and leisure than the general population of the city.

Bambi had gone to the best schools, been a debutante in the Mardi Gras court, and been a teenage star on the many local community theater stages. It just seemed destiny that one day when a movie production company was shooting a film in New Orleans that Bambi would win a role.

They were searching for a local teenager to play a major part opposite two big Hollywood A-list actors. It also won her a best supporting actress Academy Award. So, after high school graduation, she skipped college and moved to Hollywood and the rest is history.

As Bambi drove her car down the private road into the swamp, she was thinking about all the years with her boys. Doreen rode with her because the babies were safe in the child safety seats in the back seat. Arty followed in his pickup truck behind them.

Doreen felt awkward, Bambi had hardly spoken a word
to her. They did not know each other well. Doreen
didn't think Bambi approved of her. And, in truth,
Bambi didn't. The last place in the world Bambi had
wanted her son to end up was on a farm in Louisiana.

Bambi loved coming home to Louisiana as a retreat, but
Hollywood was now her home. Doreen was not the kind
of girl Bambi had pictured for Arty. But over the last
two days, unknown to Doreen, Bambi had changed her
mind about her.

Doreen impressed her when she rescued Arty from jail.
Shocked when she discovered Doreen had served two
tours of duty in the war, she realized this girl might be
what Arty needed to keep him out of trouble. They sure
seemed to be deeply in love with each other.

Bambi realized she had never experienced real love. She
felt glad one of her boys had found happiness. She had
no idea what would make Victor happy. She could not
imagine there could be a woman anywhere in the world
who would marry Victor.

"Do you miss Hollywood?" Doreen asked, trying
desperately to find some common ground with her
mother-in-law.

"Wow, do I miss it? Yes." Bambi surprised herself that
she sounded so profoundly sincere.

Doreen was a little taken aback by Bambi's being so truthful, she had expected the usual late-night show actor's usual complaints about the business.

"I actually love my job in show business," Bambi confessed. "Even though I'll admit I bitch about it a lot of times while I'm doing it. There are very frustrating things about it. But, when the camera is rolling and I become someone else, I am in the moment and it's exciting. It really is, I can't imagine anything else I could have done. Gosh, when I think that I could have ended up a housewife in New Orleans like my mother."

"I like being a housewife and a new mother." Doreen replied.

"Oh, you have no idea what being a mother is about yet. That journey has just started. And with twins! My two boys were like Yin and Yang, complete opposites. Raising them was truly the greatest role of my life."

Doreen burst into tears. "I just wanted a simple life on the farm."

"Well, that's never going to happen. I can tell you that right now. But don't cry. You have a right to be scared." Bambi comforted her or at least tried. "But, honestly Doreen, darling, from what I have learned about you in the last two days I don't believe you really yearned for a simple life on a farm."

"Any young girl who joins the Marines and does two tours of duty in a war," Bambi continued as she swerved to miss a hole in the road. "I mean okay. You did the first one maybe not knowing what you had gotten yourself into and survived it. Then you decided to go back into combat? That takes guts, determination, and a yearning for adventure."

Doreen laughed, realizing it was true.

"Heck, you had a simple life on a farm, and you chose to leave it. When you came back you left it again. I think you and Arty are perfect for each other. In his heart Arty longs for adventure too. Believe me, you two are about to go on a lifetime of adventures with these two kids. It's not going to be easy. But you're up to the challenge."

"I'm glad you think so. I'm not so sure."

"Yes, you are. You're sure."

Doreen felt so much better now. The ice was broken, and they chatted like friends. Bambi was so relieved and happy too. All she ever wanted was for her sons to be happy. She would do anything for her grandchildren too. She had never been cast in a sci-fi adventure film before, but she felt life had just put her into one. This was real life, not acting. Real life, she kept thinking to herself as she drove down further into the swamp.

Doreen kept telling her war stories that had actually happened to her. Nobody had ever wanted to hear her stories. She enjoyed telling them to Bambi.

They arrived at the get-away camp and the canopy of the forest opened up onto a panorama of a sprawling body of water. Trees were silhouetted by the glorious glow of the red ball sun as it slowly edged down in the sky. It cast a beautiful, orange and purple glow on the still water of the swamp that was snuggled deep into Cajun country.

What Doreen saw was a rustic, yet very comfortable-looking fishing camp house hanging out over the water with a pier and a porch surrounding it on all sides. What Bambi saw were memories and the relief that they were safe. What Arty saw was home.

The sounds of a swamp were never-ending. They were constant: mosquitoes buzzed, frogs croaked, and an occasional pelican squawked.

The first thing Bambi did was start spraying herself from head to foot with a green can of bug spray, then, she handed it to Doreen. "Spray yourself and keep that can, you're going to need it. And don't worry I packed a whole case in the trunk. We're covered. Day or night, down here, the skeeters never stop biting."

Bambi's car and Arty's pickup truck were parked on the side in a gravel parking area with a gravel road leading into the cypress forest. Bambi helped Arty unload their truck. Doreen tended to Scooter and Willow.

"Those stupid cops, they'll never find you out here," Bambi told them. "This is my own little private getaway. Although I may have a mansion in Beverly Hills, an apartment in the French Quarter that everybody knows about, this place is off their radar."

Doreen was impressed. "I love it. But I wish we could have stayed at my family farm."

"You can never go back to your farm. That is the first place they will look." Bambi told her.

"I can't believe I'm a wanted man. A criminal hunted by the law." Arty protested as he took suitcases out of the back of the truck and set them on the ground.

"You're not a criminal," Doreen assured him. "I'm the criminal."

"Better get those babies inside before the skeeters eat them up," Bambi instructed her. "I already put up a baby bed in the main bedroom. As a grandmother, I knew you would be out here sooner or later. I didn't expect twins, so they'll have to share it."

"At least I met some nice fellas in jail," Arty said, not listening to his mother.

She looked at him as Doreen and the babies rushed inside. "Honestly, Arty, you can get along with anybody. You always have."

"I couldn't get along with that judge. He was a mean old thing."

"I'll handle Judge Wifflestein. I know quite a few tales about him I could tell that would get him disbarred."

She and Arty carried suitcases to the porch as Doreen exited the house without the babies.

"The babies are happily in their new home. Here let me help with those. I'm not pregnant anymore. I can finally help with stuff again."

"I'll get it," Arty told her. "Enjoy the view at sunset."

Doreen looked out over the bayou as birds flew across the sky. "It's really beautiful out here."

"And peaceful," Bambi added as she carried bags of groceries into the house. Arty exited and headed back out to his truck.

"Isn't this place great?" Arty exclaimed as he carried a box from the truck. "Be careful of the gators though. The ones out here aren't vegans like our friendly Granddaddy Gator. He's become my pet. Remember the time Victor tried to feed me to the gators, Mama?"

"They refused to hurt you," Bambi told Doreen as she exited the kitchen and headed back to her car.

"That's because I communicate with them. They really don't like the taste of humans." Arty told them as suddenly, the "mew mew" sounds of hungry baby kittens were heard.

"You brought the cats?" Doreen asked as she looked in the box.

Arty carried the box with the cat and kittens up the pier to the main house. "Of course, Miss Tootsie always sleeps with me, she would have driven your mom and Grandpa crazy all night. Mister Jasper will miss me, but he won't bother them because I've been away from him before. But, gosh I'm gonna miss my horse, no tellin' how long we may be out here hiding." He went inside with Miss Tootsie and her kittens.

"I hope the police don't interrogate Mama and Grandpa too much." Doreen fretted.

"Your mama can take care of herself. Besides, neither one of them knows where this place is." Bambi told her. "So, what can they tell the cops? And don't worry it's not a war zone, so, they can't torture them."

The fishing camp was a bit rustic and old, but it was very comfortably furnished with a double bed and carpet on the bedroom floor. That's where Arty placed Miss

Tootsie and her three-day-old kittens under a small deco nightstand with a Tiffany lamp.

The kids were sleeping in a portable crib near the screened window. A nice breeze blew the sheer curtains. The room had a great view of the sunset over the water and Arty relaxed, feeling at home here.

He took a minute to look at the familiar view and make a note of any changes he spotted. He was amazed that it was all the same really, almost nothing had changed. Things change slowly in a swamp unless there is a hurricane and this area had been lucky lately.

He saw a few boards off the boathouse and some bent tin on its roof. He would have to go check on the boats in the morning he thought to himself and headed into the kitchen.

The kitchen had all a kitchen needed but had not been remodeled since the nineteen-eighties. To Bambi, it desperately needed remodeling because she had memories of a similar kitchen set on a sitcom, she starred in that flopped. Arty thought it was perfect because it had always looked the same to him.

Doreen and Bambi were unloading groceries. Of course, Doreen didn't know where to put anything and Bambi would point where something went, and Doreen would put it there. She knew there was nothing worse than being in another woman's kitchen and misplacing stuff.

Her mother was extremely strict about where everything went in her kitchen and Doreen thought about how Bambi was just like that too. Besides that, she hadn't found her mother and Bambi to have very much in common.

"I'd hate to run out of groceries way out here," Doreen was concerned, "that was a long drive."

"I think you have enough for a few weeks," Bambi assured her. Arty entered the kitchen just in time to hear his mother.

"You think we'll have to be out here that long?"

"I don't know, sugar. It depends on how seriously the law takes those charges. Your wife did blow up the county jail."

"See, we're both outlaws in our hideaway. How romantic." Doreen tousled Arty's hair.

"Well, I don't know about you two but, I'm ready for bed. This has been a long few days." Arty yawned.

Bambi couldn't help but think to herself quietly that men were such babies they were always sleepy. Of course, Arty had been arrested, gone to court, thrown into jail, busted out by his wife, ridden several miles together on his horse to the farm, loaded the truck and car, and then driven two hours to get here.

So, she decided he probably could use some sleep. "You two get some rest. I'm going to sit out on the deck for a while. I'm all set up in the guest room." She walked outside.

They went into the bedroom. Doreen and Arty stood by the crib watching the babies sleep. Doreen was a proud mama, but Arty seemed concerned.

"Ain't they sweet?" Doreen purred.

Arty reached out, he tried to make himself touch Scooter. He couldn't do it. "I'm upset about their color. It's going to be tough on them. I wish they would have been normal."

"Oh, Arty. You're impossible." She covered the babies with a blanket. "Be grateful they're safe, they're healthy and they are ours."

"None of this has turned out like I expected. Look at everything we've been through in two days. And I don't think life is ever going to get better. They'll never be normal, you know."

"Nobody wants to be normal. Do they, my little sugar dumplings? No. Everybody wants to be special. Daddy Zapper, zapping folks, electrifying them, he's special. He just doesn't accept it. Aw, look, they are sleeping so close together. I guess they thought I was telling them a bedtime story, instead of the truth."

"You thought it was exciting when we first met. My touch I mean."

"Still can be. At the right time."

He went to touch her. Stopped himself. He smiled. "You need a bolt of juice, Baby? Light your fire! I'm feeling a power surge."

Doreen pointed to the lamp. "Oh no. That lamp is on your side of the bed, we know you can't turn it off without blowing the bulb, we'll have to switch sides."

"That was a quick change of subject, honey, does that mean the electricity is over between us?"

"You wake these babies and there will be fireworks." she teased.

He turned on all his charm. "One kiss. Just one kiss."

"You know where one kiss leads."

As they got closer a few sparks began to fly between their lips as they kissed. "Not so bad, huh?"

She grabbed him. They really kissed. They fell onto the bed which fell apart with a loud crash.

And the babies woke up crying. It was over.

"Aw shucks!" Arty complained.

Doreen was off of the bed and hurried over to the crib. "Now, you've done it. Grab your son."

Arty got up, looked at the baby, and backed away.

"Uh uh, not me."

"Grab Scooter and pat him like I'm patting Willow. Arty he's your child too. If you think I'm going to tend to these babies by myself, you're crazy. Grab Scooter."

"Can't do it. Can't touch 'em. Still charged up."

"Arty."

"No. I'm not touching him."

Bambi called from the deck. "Everything okay in there?"

"Yes, ma'am," Arty quickly responded.

"It's not okay, Arty. You're still blaming me for their color!"

"Well, it's not my fault." Arty disputed.

She turned on him with both crying babies in her arms. He moved further away.

"Nothing's ever your fault. Zapper!"

"Kids in school will bully them."

"I'll homeschool 'em."

"What can you teach them?"

"How to shoot a shotgun, beat the dickens out of anyone who bullies 'em, and not to marry a zapper!"

"They'll be laughed at."

"Zapper!"

"Called satanic voodoo babies."

"They've already been called that on TV."

"This is not my fault. Even if my daddy was greenish."

"Greenish?" She was shocked. This was news to her.

He stormed out in frustration.

"Oh, Arty. Come back and fight like a man."

He called his mama to help him. "Mama, will you explain to her about daddy being greenish?"

Chapter 19

Snake In The Grass

Victor was driving the WWPU van down through the wooded area of the swamp.

Winebombs sat at the controls watching the monitors as Doreen's last words were heard.

"This woman is so clueless," Winebombs responded to Doreen and Arty's discussion, "Where are we headed?"

"Mama's hideout on the river. She used to bring us out here when we were kids. I knew this is where she would bring them."

"She still doesn't know you're here."

"No. I'm sure she thinks no one will find them way out here. Surprise Mama, surprise."

At that moment the face of Quegor appeared on the monitor. Winebombs screamed and jumped away.

Quegor spoke in a husky voice. "Do what you must do!"

Victor pulled off the side of the road into the ditch and turned off the headlights. "We're almost there. I'm not going to drive down there and let them know we are here."

Victor unscrewed an electrical plug, then stuck his finger in the exposed socket.

"What are you doing?" Winebombs shrieked.

"What I was just told to do, using my abilities."

The juice started bolting through him. He sizzled in glee as electricity shot through his body sending lightning flashing throughout the van. He lit up. Sparks flashed.

She panicked. "Oh, no."

He hissed as his shape changed. She looked down at her feet. He was now a glowing poisonous snake. He slithered out the door before Winebombs could stop him.

"Be careful sir!"

The snake crawled furiously through the swamp grass towards the house. His glow could hardly be seen through the underbrush and weeds. He got closer and closer.

He crawled across the gravel parking lot, under Arty's truck and then under his mother's sports car. He raised his head like a cobra looking towards the house. He crawled up the wooden steps and crept across the back porch slowly, carefully.

He saw Arty and Doreen walking around his mother's usual bedroom. He found them! Suddenly he realized his mother Bambi was on the back porch cleaning her shotgun. He must be careful that she did not see him in this form.

Doreen placed a sleeping Willow back in her bed.

Arty, timidly entered with a saucer of milk for the cat and her kittens. Now they were in a comfortable bed under the twin's bed.

"We still don't know what's really going on here. I wish I'd read that baby book you gave me." Arty said.

"Too late now." Doreen told him. It wouldn't have helped you. You have to be willing to touch babies if you're gonna take care of them. You touched them when they were born."

"I'm still not too sure about that."

The snake coiled over to the window and looked up at them through the glass as Arty and Doreen changed clothes for bed.

Victor slithered back to where Bambi was now watching a movie on her notebook with her shotgun by her side. A tea kettle whistle blew on the stove in the kitchen. She headed into the kitchen leaving the back door ajar. The snake saw his chance, crawled up onto the porch, and followed behind her unseen.

She went to the stove, turned off the kettle, and started making a cup of hot tea. The snake crawled inside, under the table. She turned thinking she had heard something. Victor stopped and coiled. "Does she sense my presence?" he wondered to himself. She stopped at the table and put sugar in her tea. Victor was right by her feet.

She stood there, dipping the tea bag for a long time, constantly looking around her. She felt something odd. She did not know what. Something felt strange but she shrugged it off and sipped her tea. The snake did not move. She headed out and closed the back door. Victor crawled across the floor and into the bedroom.

Arty was in his pajamas, he took off his socks and threw them under the bed. He did not see the snake crawl into the room behind him. He walked barefoot to the closet and put his shoes inside. Then, he turned as the snake headed towards the bed.

"You think somebody, somewhere, can help our kids? I mean we got to do something, right?" He asked Doreen who was now dressed for bed brushing her teeth in the bathroom.

"Accept and love them the way they are. Don't try to change them," she mumbled with her mouth full of toothpaste. She quickly grabbed a paper cup and gargled then spit. She went back into the bedroom and hung her dress on a wire hanger in the closet.

The snake on the floor saw Arty's bare feet right in front of him. One bite and his brother would be out of the picture. All it would take was one quick bite. He made his move and slithered quickly across the floor towards Arty's feet, his fangs ready to strike.

"If we don't do something, Doreen, we will regret it later." Arty sighed as he moved, and the snake missed him and slithered under the bed.

Victor coiled again and got ready. He had been so close, so close!

Arty and Doreen's bare feet could be seen as they stood beside the bed.

"Do we really need to know the truth? Or the reason why?" she asked.

Arty paced the floor quicker and quicker. The snake watched every move from under the bed.

The cat Miss Tootsie, on the floor across the room, had finished the milk. She suddenly seemed to notice and sense that something was not quite right.

Arty went over to Doreen. "Darling, we're always arguing now."

"Can't you accept your own flesh and blood? What's wrong with you Arty? You've become heartless."

"Heartless!"

The snake under the bed stuck out his fangs, his muscles moved as he got closer and closer to Arty's feet. Just then, Doreen's feet moved closer to Arty's. The snake stopped and coiled. He did not want to bite her by mistake. He wanted Doreen for himself.

"You used to be the kindest person I ever knew. I mean, you saved a spider so the mayor wouldn't step on it."

Arty moved away, the snake tried to strike and missed again. It slithered between the two of them.

"You just called me heartless. What happened to doodles dumpling?"

"You are not my doodles dumpling anymore."

They were both clueless about what was happening on the floor around them until the cat hissed.

Victor coiled.

The naked feet continued to move around him. When the snake lunged towards Arty's feet the cat pounced. Victor felt the cat's claws rip into his snake body. The pain was intense.

Arty stepped away just in time and the snake missed him. The cat accidentally struck Arty's ankle with her claws this time.

He reacted in pain. "Miss Tootsie!"

"Oh, she's upset over some snake on the floor." Doreen countered, still obsessed with their argument.

"Snake?" Arty jumped and backed into the table and knocked over his mama's favorite lamp. It crashed onto the floor scaring both the cat and the snake who raced in opposite directions as sparks flew from the breaking bulb.

Suddenly, the snake stopped, Victor realized Arty was standing right by him and the snake reared his head ready to strike.

Doreen sensed something. She looked down and saw the snake now ready to bite Arty. "There's the snake. Watch your feet."

Arty jumped around like a scared child and called his Mama. "Mama! Bring your shotgun."

On the porch, Bambi heard him and jumped up spilling her hot tea. She put down her notebook, grabbed her shotgun, and headed into the bedroom.

"What's going on in here?" she asked as she entered.

Doreen pointed to the floor. "Snake. Shoot him."

Bambi saw it. Shot. Missed.

The snake crawled fast as lightning across the floor and into the closet. Arty slammed the door.

"Let's run," he shouted.

In the van, Winebombs watched on her monitors and screamed. Then bolted out of her chair. "They've shot the doctor." She grabbed the biggest gun she could find and ran out of the van, down the road towards the house.

Bambi had her gun pointed at the closet, she carefully inched towards the door.

"Don't be a baby." She barked at Arty. "Open the door slowly and I'll blow it to smithereens."

Arty was too scared. "I hate snakes."

Doreen opened the door. Bambi aimed.

Both recoiled as a human Victor fell out of the closet. There was a wire clothes hanger stuck around his neck. The snake's head went through the hanger as he morphed, and it was now lodged around his human throat.

"No wire hangers," he wailed. He landed at their feet desperately trying to bend the hanger over his face so he could get free of it.

"Victor? What were you doing in the closet son?"

Victor, in shock, looked up at her.

"Mommie Dearest?" He cried.

Winebombs kicked down the door and burst into the kitchen with a bazooka pointed at the bedroom and rushed inside, "Get away from the doctor or I'll blow this shack to New Orleans," she threatened.

"Who are you?" Bambi inquired, shocked and confused.

Winebombs went to Victor. "Oh, my darling, Sir. Who did this to you? I'll blow their brains out!"

She pointed her gun at Bambi. "Was it you?"

"Don't kill her, that's my mother" Victor ordered quickly.

Winebombs pointed her bazooka at Arty. "Was it you?"

"That's my brother."

Sure now, Winebombs points at Doreen. "Then, it was you!"

"Nooo, that's my girlfriend!"

Arty, Bambi, and Winebombs are stunned. They all three blurted out at the same time,

"Girlfriend?"

That made up Winebomb's mind. "Then, she's the one I'm killing!"

Victor stopped her. "No—I love her."

Arty was destroyed. He turned to Doreen, "Is that true?"

"It's over. Long ago." She turned to Victor. "You had to tell, you heartless snake! I left you in Afghanistan!"

She ran out crying. Arty headed out to Doreen.

"Mommie, the devil made me do it," Victor whimpered, reaching out and touching his mother's shoes.

Winebombs tried to help Victor, "Let me get this wire thing over your head, Sir, and clean you up. You got all dirty crawling through that dirt."

Arty followed Doreen out to the yard in a huff. He charged over to her. "Did you marry me because I looked like my brother?"

"Go away, Arty, not now. I have to be alone to think."

"Yes, now!"

She was surprised at him. "Arty? You've never yelled at me"

"I want the truth now! Don't be a marine about it. Be a lady."

"I thought you were him when I first saw you in that grocery store."

"That's why you slapped me, kicked me, threw me to the ground, and started beating me? I thought it was love at first sight!"

"I thought you were Victor. I hated him so much I wanted to kill him. When I realized you weren't him, I was so embarrassed that I ran away."

"Hit and run, always been my policy too. Well, Doreen, you have always been a gal who got what she wanted, so why me?"

She didn't even have to think about it for a moment because she knew the answer. "You turned out to be so kind, so loving, the total opposite of him and yet in the looks department you were the same hunk."

Arty was shocked when he realized. "I'm a hunk?"

"Yes, Arty, look in the mirror, you're a hunk."

Arty was amazed. "When did that happen?"

She grabbed him and kissed him passionately. "Oh, Arty, you're so sweet, so innocent, I love you so much."

"You do? You don't love him? He said he loved you."

"He's a horrible monster. You have no idea how horrible. You're my doodles dumpling."

They kissed again. Sparks started to fly. Then, Bambi walked up and interrupted them.

"Uh, excuse me, lovebirds, but I think maybe you might want to talk to your brother about the babies."

"Why would I want to talk to that snake? He tried to kill me." Arty snapped angrily.

Bambi continued, "The reason they are here is to help the babies. Victor has a government lab, especially for people with special abilities."

"He wants to experiment on our babies. That fake Doctor Bobo said so. We won't do it. Victor and all his other goons are evil."

Suddenly, Winebombs appeared with her bazooka. "You don't really have a choice, people. We have a plane ready and waiting back at the airport. This plan was put in place months ago. You are a part of this whether you like it or not. And I've got the biggest gun."

Chapter 20
Up Up & Away

An airplane zoomed through dark, foreboding clouds. Inside the plane, Doreen and the twins were fast asleep in the front section. They were guarded by Doctor Bobo on one side and Trumbo on the other.

Arty sat on the aisle seat next to Dana LaFoosie who sat by the window. Victor sat across from Arty with Winebombs by his side.

A flight attendant passed out coffee and pastries. She spoke to Doctor Bobo. "Coffee? Pastry?"

Doctor Bobo looked around him to make sure no one was paying attention, then he whispered to her. "Any donuts? Jelly filled donuts?"

"Sure sugar," she replied with a southern drawl so slow, so sweet, it was molasses covering buttered pancakes. "Here's a whole box of lemon ones. How many do you want.?"

"I'll take the whole box," he whispered.

"Okay, sugar." She handed him the donuts.

Winebombs yelled from her seat. "Doctor Bobo! Put those back."

He handed them back to the flight attendant. "Maybe later, save me some."

She continued down the aisle. "Coffee? Pastry?"

A computer nerd worked on a laptop, then handed Victor a disk. "Here's all the data you requested, Sir. There seems to be an odd, worldwide cosmic event happening. It may be connected to the birth of these twins."

"Interesting," Victor said as he took the disk. "Keep me updated." He recognized the young man but could not place the face. "What is your name again?"

"Purvis sir, Private Leroy Purvis."

Suddenly, Victor remembered him. "Oh, yes, you are Doctor Bobo's patient. I remember you from the lab. Good to have you onboard with our program. I assume you are cured of your fear of aliens?"

"Oh, yes, sir. Completely cured. Monsters only exist in my imagination. I realize that now. I'm not afraid of anything now, Sir"

"Glad to hear it. That will be all." Victor dismissed him with a smile.

Leroy gave Dana LaFoosie the eye, as he headed towards the restroom at the back of the plane. He gave her one more look before he closed the door and did not lock it. She noticed, but she wasn't interested.

Arty spoke to Dana. He was completely oblivious to the interchange between her and Leroy. "Do you think they serve nuts? I get nervous on planes. I wish that woman would hurry down here with the refreshments. I feel better when I'm eating and drinking something."

Dana did not speak, she just smiled. It was amazing to her how much Arty and Victor looked alike yet were so different. She found Victor to be a sadistic beast with extremely refined taste and this Arty guy next to her was so innocent and pleasant. She knew if she said anything Victor would punish her.

"I always enjoyed you on that game show. It was Victor's favorite. It's a shame it got canceled." She smiled again. He had no idea how insulting his compliment was to a has-been like her.

Winebombs looked over her seat at the twins in front of her. This annoyed Doreen who coughed and gave her the eye. Scooter opened one eye and gave her his little middle finger.

"That baby just shot me the bird!" Winebombs exclaimed in shock.

"You're crazy! He's only three days old."

"He's the bad one."

"Neither of my children are bad. Will you please sit back? You're annoying me."

"You wait. Time will tell. I am always right. He's the bad one." Winebombs laughed as she sat back in her seat.

Lightning flashed across the sky. A major electrical storm was brewing outside.

Turbulence jolted the plane. The passengers reacted when the fasten seatbelt sign turned on as the flight attendant's voice came over the loudspeaker. She talked into a microphone even though she was standing right in front of them on this very small plane.

"The Captain has turned on the fasten seat belt sign, all passengers please return to your seats." She announced sweet as a Georgia peach.

A bright light flashed outside the window as several streaks of lightning zoomed across the darkening sky. There was a loud boom of thunder. The plane shook as the storm hit.

"Oh no." Arty warned Dana, "Stay calm, there's no reason to panic. I don't always get struck by lightning every time. Sometimes it misses me."

She had no idea what he was talking about. "What?" she replied.

The plane rocked and shook like a roller coaster. Tension started to build on all the passengers' faces as they scrambled to buckle up.

Doreen tended to the babies who were awake and crying. "Everything okay back there Arty?"

"Yes, sugar dumpling. So far, so good."

Victor smirked. "Sugar dumpling? Make me vomit."

Doreen ignored Victor's smarmy remark and continued her conversation with Arty. "Keep it that way." Doreen warned, referring to Arty's relationship with lightning. "It's okay," she whispered to her children, and she started humming a song to calm them down.

The flight attendant wobbled down the aisle to her station and also buckled up.

When she walked past. Arty said to Dana. "I never got any peanuts," Their eyes locked in a dead freeze. Their corneas flashed lightning. They connected on a visceral level. Arty suddenly recognized her, "I know where I saw you before. You were the Vegas showgirl in our front yard. I never did get my motivational DVDs."

"She is my assistant. That whole wise people charade was a made-up scam by the government to get cameras into your house, stupid. There were no DVDs. Isn't that right Sugar Dumpling?" Victor lied intimating that there was a romance between him and Dana.

Dana was completely confused by both of them, and her smile showed it. "Huh," she answered, certain that sugar dumpling did not apply to her situation with Victor.

Arty looked into her eyes again. "How could you work with this man? He has been mean and cruel since we were in the womb together." He turned to Victor adamantly, "Doreen and the babies are mine and they will never be yours."

Victor snapped back. "We'll see about that. She loved me first and she'll love me again when she realizes what a weakling you are."

Right next to Arty, a blinding bolt of lightning flashed through the darkening clouds and struck the wing of the plane with a loud boom. Arty's temper was building.

Dana could see the lightning in his eyes, and it scared her, but she could not look away. She felt danger. The power in Arty's eyes mesmerized her and reminded her of Ol' Lightning back in Victor's lab.

Winebombs jumped up and rushed to the other restroom, "I'm gonna be sick", she exclaimed, her face all snarled in an attempt to hold it until the toilet.

The tips of Arty's fingers started to sparkle. His hair started to rise slowly, it looked like Albert Einstein's hair. It began floating in mid-air.

Suddenly, a flash of electrical current zapped out of Arty's fingers and jumped from seat to seat, bolting down the aisle, both ways. Everyone reacted like they were shocked. The plane was electrified.

Arty grabbed Dana's hand and could not let go. "Sorry, I have to hold on to someone or I'll explode!"

She bolted upright in her seat as his electricity flew into her as it did inside Ol' Lightning. She was the one who was about ready to explode. Dana sizzled.

Within seconds the entire interior of the plane was buzzing with hissing current. Every person on board was shaking in their seats like prisoners in electric chairs. Their hair started frizzing and standing high on their heads as the current zapped through each hair.

"Arty, you are giving everybody a perm!" Doreen shrieked.

Dana started to foam at the mouth. She knew what that meant. She pushed past Arty and rushed down the aisle to the restrooms. When she got there both were occupied. She panicked as she knocked furiously on the door.

Inside Leroy, the young nerd sat on the tiny toilet with his pants around his ankles. The computer was on his lap as he read the news. He reacted to the pounding on the door. "Just a sec," he responded, but Dana pulled on the door, and it was unlocked. She pushed inside. Leroy's eyes filled with excitement. "Oh, yeah baby, Mile High Club!"

Suddenly, Dana's face started to turn purple. Her teeth grew long, her dragon-like elongated face emerged. Leroy screamed as she started licking him with her long pink tongue.

Dana looked down at the tablet screen in his lap and saw something on the news. She grabbed the computer away from him and stared at the screen. On the screen, a purple Sally Ann was singing and tap dancing on a video. Dana got very hungry.

Inside the cabin, the plane rocked violently.

At his seat, Arty reached across the aisle, grabbed Victor's hand, and could not let go. The current shot into Victor full force. He screamed as his body twisted and contorted in agony. Victor started to hiss and transformed into the glowing poisonous snake.

Arty suddenly realized his hand was empty. The snake crawled down the aisle towards the kids' seat. The twins, now wide awake, stared at the coiled snake. Doreen was frozen in fear.

Arty stood and wobbled his way towards the snake as the plane rocked from violent turbulence. "Don't move Doreen! I don't have my snake bite kit!"

"Oh, no. It's Victor the snake again!" She realized at once.

Arty grabbed the snake and wrestled it down the aisle. The snake hissed and bit at him. Arty was electrocuting it with his mighty powers as he rushed down the aisle towards the bathroom.

He got to the restroom, opened the door, and saw the purple monster with Leroy. He slammed that door shut.

The opposite restroom door opened and Winebombs exited. She was trying to push down her pink hair which looked like a wad of cotton candy. She saw Arty and the snake. She screeched. "Not again Doctor!"

"Move it!" Arty pushed Winebombs out of his way. He beat the snake hard against the restroom wall.

"Don't hurt the doctor!" Winebombs cried out.

Arty banged the snake on the sink a couple of times. Victor hissed and spit poison. It was war between brothers.

In total terror, Winebombs stood transfixed, watching. Arty lifted the seat cover and threw the snake into the toilet and flushed twice. Doreen rushed towards Arty and saw what he was doing.

Winebombs stood between them crying. "You flushed the doctor down the toilet."

Arty backed out as she rushed in. "He deserved it."

Doreen grabbed her man and hugged him. "Oh, Arty, you were wonderful! You saved us. My hero."

Arty was very concerned. Something inside him had changed forever. "Are my babies okay? No one is taking them away from us. I'm fed up, and when I'm fed up, that's it, I'm fed up!"

"Calm down. Don't blow up the plane," she warned him.

He calmed himself and rushed back down the aisle and quickly picked up Scooter who was crying and hugged him.

"Did that terrible ol' snake, your Uncle Victor, scare you? He's gone where all the bad things go, down the toilet." The baby stopped crying at the loving touch of his father.

"Arty, look, you did it. You overcame your fear."

"No one is harming my children."

"We can't show favorites, hand me Scooter and you hug Willow."

He handed Scooter to her and picked up Willow, then hugged her gently. She stopped crying too.

"Come here little lady, give Daddy a hug. Oh, she feels like another little sugar dumpling to me. I love you, sweetheart. Don't cry. I got the power under control now."

Willow stopped crying, looked deep into her Daddy's eyes, and giggled in delight.

"Oh, Arty, now we're a normal family."

"Don't ever say that word again."

"What word?"

"Normal. Who wants to be normal? We're special."

"Oh, Arty." Doreen hugged her man.

He looked at the flight attendant. "I'm her hunk."

Suddenly in the restroom with Leroy, the purple people eater was still looking at the video of purple Sally Ann. The purple people eater was growing bigger and bigger. She burst out of the plane, ripping the metal walls creating a gaping hole in the back.

The purple people eater flew out in all her glory. Her gigantic wings soared through the air. She lifted her head and blew a long flame of fire and smoke from her mouth. She howled and broke off the wing of the plane in the process. The plane started to nosedive.

The flight attendant panicked and screamed, "I can't fly this plane!"

"I can save us." Doctor Bobo shouted as he rushed to her. "Give me that box of lemon jelly donuts." She gave it to him quickly.

Doctor Bobo grabbed the box of donuts and quickly started stuffing donut after donut into his mouth. The yellow goo started to pour from his nose, his ears, his mouth, down his legs and arms. He turned into a gigantic size yellow Glob. He started to seep under the plane door.

The goo-covered plane was headed straight down through the clouds towards the airport. Doctor Bobo, now a bigger and bigger yellow Glob, quickly covered the entire outside of the plane. The giant yellow Glob was falling to earth.

Darkness overwhelmed the inside of the plane, as the windows became covered with yellow goo. It dripped down on the passengers. The interior of the plane started falling apart. The Glob was the only thing holding it together.

Outside, the ever-expanding Glob fell through the sky as it stretched out to engulf the entire airplane. The face of Doctor Bobo could be seen at the head of the plane over the cockpit.

Enjoying every moment of the excitement, "Yippee!" he crowed until he reached earth. Then, The Glob hit the ground; it rolled like jello and then bounced. Boing! Boing! Boing! Towards the airport.

Everyone was upside down inside, rolling over and over like a carnival ride. The passengers screamed, except for the babies, who giggled like two kids on a Ferris wheel. They were having another adventure.

The Glob rolled down the runway. Planes squealed as they turned off the runway into the grass to miss the giant yellow thing rolling towards them. Doctor Bobo started moaning like a man who ate too many donuts.

The moaning goo covered plane pulled into the airport gate. The ground workers driving various vehicles went racing about to get out of the way. The goo rolled off the plane and morphed again into its human form, Doctor Bobo. He stood and gathered himself, totally normal now, and walked into the airport.

Chapter 21

Koolidoscope Kids

Inside the plane, everything was still covered in yellow dripping goo. The flight attendant tried to remain calm as she spoke into her microphone.

"The plane has safely landed. Please remain seated until the seat belt sign is turned off."

She swiped a big blob of goo off of her face and slung it to the floor. "Oh, forget the seat belt sign, get your stuff and get out of here."

Arty, Doreen, and the twins emerged from the doorway of the plane. They walked down the ramp to the inside of the airport leaving yellow goo behind them.

It was a very modern airport interior with television screens everywhere flashing the news of the hour. Nobody paid any attention to the family because everyone was transfixed on the screens. Arty looked up and reacted to what he saw. "Look, it's our mayor."

On the newscast, a commentator stood next to Mayor Weidican and a sobbing purple Sally Ann. Her skin was blotchy in spots, but she was still very purple.

"Mayor Weidican of Rainbow City admitted the whole "alien" saga was a giant hoax. It was cooked up by little Sally Ann Dingledorper who had dyed herself purple with clothes dye."

"Look Arty. Everyone thinks it was fake news." Doreen elbowed him and smiled.

"That's good news for us. Cover the babies, so no one sees their color."

Harper, Victor's car attendant, approached Arty and saluted. He thought Arty was Victor. He would have had no way of knowing there was a twin brother. Harper saluted "Transport right this way, Doctor Wood, Sir. Your car is waiting and there's a bus for the others."

Doreen and Arty froze at first, then an idea crossed Arty's mind. He spoke to Harper, imitating Victor's voice and manner. "About time, soldier." Arty saluted back. Then, he announced to Doreen with a courtly bow, "Your chariot awaits, my lady."

Harper recognized that game type of talk right away. "Yes, sir. Follow me, sir. I'm afraid I don't know where that quote came from, Sir. Sorry."

"Julius Caesar, third act." Arty made it up quickly. Doreen, confused, looked at Arty like he was crazy. He shrugged and explained, "A little guessing game we play." Doreen shook her head and realized he and Victor must have played this game as children.

Harper led them through the airport to Victor's red sports car. They tried not to be overly impressed, but they were very impressed.

"Your car, as ordered, sir. I'll drive the others to the base in the military van." He handed Arty the keys. Arty took them quickly before the gig was up. "And open the door for the lady." he demanded, "She has her hands full with the babies."

"Of course, sir." Harper rushed to the other side of the car and opened the door for Doreen.

Doreen was surprised to see car seats in place.

"There are already car seats for the babies?"

"Oh, yes ma'am. I was given detailed instructions on the care of the babies. We've been expecting them for weeks now. You'll find everything ready for the experiments at the compound."

Then he saw the babies and his eyes grew wide with excitement. "The turquoise twins" he exclaimed. "How wonderful."

Arty quickly responded. "Quiet soldier, this is a secret mission!"

"Oh, I'm so sorry, sir. Of course."

Doreen put the babies in the seats with help from Harper, then she got in the front seat.

"Have you gone nuts?" she whispered to Arty.

He quickly hushed her. Then he turned to Harper and said, "May the Force be with you."

"And also with you, Sir," Harper groveled to Arty as he closed the back door. He was so excited. "Star Wars. Right, Sir? I got one right?"

"Bully for you, son. Bully for you." Arty replied.

Harper was beaming with joy. They saluted each other again. Arty started the car and flew out of the parking lot as fast as he could.

Inside the plane, everyone had exited the cabin except Winebombs who was still in the restroom, sobbing loudly. The flight attendant walked down the aisle and knocked on the restroom door. She was still covered in goo. She flipped a piece of it off her shoulder.

"You have to come out now. We've landed." She opened the bathroom door and saw Winebombs hugging the empty toilet bowl, crying hysterically.

"Oh, Doctor, Doctor. My poor Doctor. The man I love is in this toilet." she told the attendant.

The attendant didn't bat an eye, she simply called in a monotone voice into her cell "Security. I need security."

She calmly opened the other door. Her eyes widened. Leroy, most of his clothes shredded, gripped the toilet frozen in fear. He shook like a freezing man, his teeth chattered. The entire back section of the plane was missing.

The flight attendant calmly called again into her phone. "Maintenance. I need maintenance."

Outside the plane, the luggage handlers were unloading the luggage as the honey wagon guy drove his vehicle to the plane. The handlers looked at each other and responded to a strange banging inside the metal container beside them. "Somebody passed a lot of gas," one of them laughed to the other.

Something dripped on them. They looked up and saw yellow goo seeping from the plane. At that moment, the honey wagon driver pulled the lever to empty the toilet into the honey wagon.

A snake slithered out of the poop tank. All three men jumped out of its way and ran screaming when it shapeshifted into a very human, but very wet, smelly Victor.

Victor pulled himself up with as much dignity as he could muster. He walked towards the terminal: filthy, dripping a foul-smelling liquid and dragging a long stream of toilet paper stuck to his shoe.

At the same time the red car zoomed away from the airport fading in the distance. The babies were asleep in the car seats in the back. But one of Scooter's eyes opened. He watched the news flash on the television screen in the car.

Inside the airport, the news flashed on every screen. Victor stopped and stared at them. The people around him suddenly smelled him. Some gagged, a few threw up. Everyone ran to get away from him as soon as possible. He did not move. He just stared at the screens.

The caption running across the screen read RAINBOW COLORED BABIES BEING BORN ACROSS THE WORLD.

In the car, Doreen and Arty watched the same news. "Wouldn't it have been easier for us to fly back home?" Doreen asked, "We are somewhere near the Smoky Mountains."

"Haven't you realized yet, they're not gonna let us go home? We can't go back to Rainbow City."

"Then where are we going?"

"Not sure, yet. But there are kids like ours, but different colors, being born all over the world. We need to find them. Their parents are like us."

"Oh, boy. A road trip." Doreen exclaimed with growing excitement. "Our first adventure together as a family. We need to stop and get baby supplies. How soon you think they're gonna be on our tail."

"Soon."

"You and I've never been on an adventure together."

"I'm thinking our entire life is going to be an adventure from now on, Doreen. Thank goodness I married a Marine."

Doreen smiled. "About time you started to appreciate my military skills."

"Oh, I do, I do."

Outside the car, high in the sky above them, The Purple People Eater, flew through the air with purple Sally Ann in her claws. Sally Ann was screaming, "I'm not really purple!"

Chapter 22

Across the Globe

In the middle of the Norwegian Sea, a fishing boat was crashing through tsunami-sized waves in a furious storm. The boat's crew were being tossed around like toys while pulling in a net full of fish.

Squawking seagulls swarmed around above the boat and a school of whales danced as they harmonized in a lullaby of whale songs.

One of the crew stopped and pulled off her yellow slicker and cap, revealing that she was very pregnant. Her husband, the captain, rushed over to her and she indicated that the baby was coming. He helped her inside their cabin.

The seagulls became quiet. The whale-song ceased. The only sound was the roaring of the sea as the boat continued to crash and dip in the rough waves.

Ominously the sky blackened, and streaks of lightning flashed through the air as Quegor made his presence known. The crew quaked in fear.

Inside the cabin, the husband washed his hands in a bucket of water and got on his knees to help his wife deliver the baby.

Aquaria appeared, a swirling vortex in the sea like a giant waterspout. She pulled the ship towards her, enveloping it in water and mist. She morphed magically into a flowing liquid female form that floated into the cabin to assure the child's survival.

The sailors trembled in their rubber boots at the sight of this mythological creature on their boat. The father appeared from the cabin with a happy baby girl that was a bright coral color.

The crew attacked the captain and tied him up. They grabbed the baby and threw her into the sea.

Quegor furiously threw lightning bolt after lightning bolt until the boat exploded into a thousand pieces. sailors, lumber, nets and fish went flying in all directions. Aquaria zoomed out of what had been the cabin with the mother in her arms and rescued the baby from the waves.

A small lifeboat bobbed in the sea pushed by the dolphins, Aquaria gently placed the mother inside, then handed her the crying baby girl. A school of dolphins used their noses to push the boat away from the sinking ship.

The sailors drowned in the crashing waves. Only the captain managed to hang onto a large piece of the boat as he was swept away in a different direction than his wife and child.

A few moments later on, the other side of the world in the South Pacific Ocean, there was a small unnamed island. It's one humble village built by nomad refugees perched in the shadow of a long-dormant volcano.

A young woman in the village gave birth to a baby boy who was as red as fire. The mouth of the crater began to rumble and spewed fire and ash as Quegor raged.

Suddenly, dark smoke burst from the vents of the summit as the ground shook with a fury of an atomic bomb explosion. The fire of Quegor burst forth into the sky, a hot searing lava.

It poured down the flank of the volcano and covered the village within a second. People screamed as they melted alive in the hot lava. It devoured everything in its path until it came to the newborn baby boy.

Miraculously, the molten rock circled the hut and lifted it up with the mother and child inside. The flaming liquid carried their abode down towards the sea in a stream of steaming lava. The brutal fiery face of Quegor appeared in the smoke and flames. The mother cowered in fear and pain, but the baby squealed in delight and lifted his tiny arms towards the flames.

All at once, a cold wave of seawater crashed over the mother and child and sizzled as steam enveloped them both. Aquaria was cooling them and protecting them from the fire. The baby's skin glowed an even brighter red now and there were black burn marks on parts of his skin. He would be called a monster by some people and a savior by others.

The mother trembled in terror not understanding this magical event. The child's sterling deep blue eyes, that deep dark blue color that burns inside the hottest flames of a fire, stared straight into the non-human faces of Aquaria and Quegor. He was not afraid. The boy knew in that instant why he had been born of fire and water and what his destiny was to be.

TIME woke up and said, "Huh?"

Acknowledgments

From Hiram Taylor: co-writer

Special thanks to Hal and Cheryl Croasman at ScreenwritingU, where The Turquoise Twins script was first developed as a screenplay. Thanks to Judy Mills who suggested I should write it as a novel. The enthusiasm of ScreenwritingU's alumni group members who have shared feedback over the years has helped the project stay on track.

A shout-out to fellow novelists David Swatling and Robert Fleet for their support.

Big thanks to my friends, Jason Bergeron for his details about Louisiana life and his partner Robert Levinstein for legal advice and encouragement.

To all my New Orleans friends: Roxie Allbritton, Emily Truitt and the members of the Mardi Gras Krewe du Mishigas for their love and support.

From Lorre Brewer: co-writer

Hiram and I would like to thank Tracy Frost for the many hours she spent lovingly editing our book.

In addition Tracy not only gave her own time to randomly help with additional input in many areas whether it be on the creative or business side. Tracy also enlisted the aid of her colleagues and friends. Special thanks to Phyllis Conway who spent most of her vacation brain-storming super hero character names.

Cheryl Turner and Kelly Sharpe, your special care during the ARC process brought so much to our finished book. Cheryl Turner your continued enthusiasm and willingness to be an integral part of our core team fills us with gratitude.

Tyler Box thank you for bringing you artistic talent and calming presence to this project from day one. We can't wait to see where your gifts take you as you continue to bring your creative projects to fruition.

To my sister Trish Sloan, you have always been there for me and have bailed me out so many times and in so many ways. Many times during this process I called on you to share your professional talents, time and sisterly love to fill in those areas that baffled me. This has not been our first journey together and it will not be our last.

To my Daughter Jessica Brewer; yours is the presence that gets me through.

To my husband Greg Brewer. You make everything possible. Thank you for your willingness to support my business and creative adventures with patience and good humor. Your endless creative talents (music, quick wit and did I mention the culinary arts) informs everything that I accomplish. There are not enough words to thank you.

About the Authors

AUTHORS' STORY:

Hiram Taylor contacted Lorre Brewer about the possibility of coming on board as a producing partner for his Broadway-bound musical *Did You Ever Wish*. When Covid hit, Broadway shut down. Coincidentally one of Hiram's many writing projects The Turquoise Twins gained recognition from three screenwriting contests. Then it won the top spot in the Science Fiction category at the Los Angeles Screenwriting Awards.

A new writing partnership TAYLOR & BREWER began and together they expanded the concept and decided to take the story in a new direction. After completing *The Turquoise Twins* new script, movie production shut down as the film industry was also dealing with the pandemic.

Together they made the decision to write a series of books rather than focus on Hollywood or Broadway. Publishing would allow them to present their ideas on a broader scale to a worldwide audience. Thus was born the *KOOLIDOSCOPE KIDS* and their unusual adventurous stories.

HIRAM TAYLOR

Hiram Taylor wrote his first play at the age of eight and continued to write. Soon his plays were produced at local high schools and regional community theaters. Twenty-eight of his plays have been produced off-off-Broadway or off-Broadway in New York City and other major cities. At the age of nineteen he won the Bultman Playwriting Award, an international honor. His short stories have been published in various magazines. Hiram has worn many hats over a long career in show business. Among his many accomplishments; he was artistic director of the Taymon Welch Theatre Company in Manhattan and he directed documentary films in Los Angeles. He produced the film *Connections* in Louisiana and currently lives in New Orleans and is active in Mardi Gras Krewe, winning four awards for his float designs.

LORRE BREWER

Lorre Brewer began her career in entertainment as a member of the acclaimed Downey Children's Theatre at the age of eight. There she spent her early years being trained in all aspects of the theatrical arts until her high school graduation. From there she traveled to Hawaii and for the next four years she worked for the legendary Hawaiian entertainer Don Ho, once again gathering valuable experience. As fate would have it she spent another five years working with Sonny Golden who was the business manager for Frank Sinatra, Lucille Ball, Rowan & Martin et al. During those years and the years since she has continued to work on numerous projects in many different roles.

Also By

Made in the USA
Las Vegas, NV
05 February 2023

66920748R00150